STORMTIDE

STORMTIDE

A WEBB CARRICK MURDER MYSTERY

BILL KNOX

Constable • London

Constable & Robinson Ltd
3 The Lanchesters
162 Fulham Palace Road
London W6 9ER
www.constablerobinson.com

First published in Great Britain 1972

This edition published in Great Britain by Constable,
an imprint of Constable & Robinson Ltd, 2011

A copy of the British Library Cataloguing in Publication
data is available from the British Library

ISBN 978-1-84901-457-1

Printed and bound in the EU

1 3 5 7 9 10 8 6 4 2

PEFC
PEFC/16-33-111
CATG-PEFC-052
www.pefc.org

For Tara

Chapter One

First there was the flat, heavy bang of the gun, then what seemed like a million seabirds rose from the island's cliffs in a protesting cloud. A vast flurry of water appeared beside the shark-boat and a massive, black-backed shape lunged briefly to the surface before it dived deep. The fresh explosion of spray still gave a momentary glimpse of a great, lashing tail, then as the shape vanished, the harpoon line sang out and quivered taut while the shark-boat took the strain.

It had captured a giant. But it still had to kill – and even an average basking shark is larger than any elephant.

Half a mile of open water separated Her Majesty's Fishery Protection cruiser *Marlin* from the drama being enacted off the island. But what the men on her bridge could see was enough for them to sense the rest.

'Gawd, he's got a big 'un there,' muttered the duty helmsman, a tall, horse-faced individual with permanent catarrh. He sniffed hard, hands balanced assuredly on the wheel-spokes. 'There's more on the end of that harpoon than I'd want to know.'

'It's money,' said Webb Carrick absently, moving over to the bridge wing for a better view. Chief Officer Carrick knew the boat out there and the man certain to be in her wheelhouse. 'He'll manage. That's Dave Rother and the *Seapearl*, out of Portcoig on Skye.'

Using the bridge glasses, he brought the scene into close-up. A bulky figure was dancing excitedly at the catcher's bow gun and Carrick chuckled. Big Yogi Dunlop, always Rother's gunner, drunk or sober, recognized a bonus on the end of that straining nylon line.

But the great fish below was far from finished. Suddenly the black triangle of its sail-like back-fin cut into sight above the waves, heading in a new direction. Another moment and it vanished again as the basking shark dived in search of deep water.

It was a fight for survival, and on the fishery cruiser's deck an audience was growing. Any diversion was welcome.

Four hundred tons of slim, purposeful power with a crew of twenty-five, *Marlin* was on the second week of a routine Hebridean patrol and so far things had been uniformly dull. Even her big twin diesels throbbed in a bored murmur. The rest was overcast sky, a light but chill northerly wind and a choppy steel-blue sea. On the Scottish West Coast early afternoon in the month of June didn't always mean sunshine and rising temperatures.

The little shark-catcher, a converted Admiralty MFV, began to fall astern. Slowly, Carrick lowered the glasses and glanced ahead. *Marlin* was rounding the westerly point of the island with a long stretch of open sea before the next blob of land broke the horizon.

'Well, mister?' A familiar voice rasped surprisingly close to his ear and he turned. Small and stout, bearded moon-like face set in a peevish scowl, Captain James Shannon had obviously padded up from his day-cabin in a trouble-seeking mood.

Hauling himself up into the bridge command chair, legs dangling, *Marlin*'s master sniffed heavily. 'Finished enjoying the scenery?'

'Watching the *Seapearl* to port, sir,' answered Carrick, unperturbed. 'She's caught herself another shark – a big one.'

'The biggest shark around is the crook who owns that tub,' grunted Shannon, then caught a sideways glimpse of the grin which crossed the helmsman's face. 'You. Watch that course, damn you. We're not on a picnic.'

Flushing, the helmsman ironed all expression from his face, quickly eased the wheel, and stared ahead.

Shannon scowled at him for a moment. Senior captain in the Fishery Protection squadron, the bearded sixty-year-old could always make up in wrath what he lacked in size.

'I'll take over, mister,' he announced unexpectedly. 'Extra look-outs on the bridge in fifteen minutes. Until then we'll maintain course and speed.'

'Sir?' Carrick raised a mildly questioning eyebrow.

'Some damned aeroplane pilot flying out to Barra reported seeing what he thought was an oil-slick a few miles north of us.' Shannon hunched deeper into the command chair. 'Probably the sun broke through and caught some oily bilge that'll have vanished long before we get there. But there's a signal from Department saying take a look. I've told Wills to get the sprays ready for rigging, so make sure he isn't making a mess of it.'

'Aye aye, sir.' Carrick left him, grimacing once he was past the little chartroom behind the bridge.

The detergent sprays, large hose-booms, had been added to *Marlin*'s equipment at the end of her last patrol. Ever since, Shannon had regarded them as a

3

personal insult for what they did to the trim, destroyer-like lines of his 180-foot charge.

Reaching the main deck, Carrick headed aft. The shark-boat and her quarry had vanished behind the island, but there was plenty of activity getting under way at *Marlin*'s stern, where the distinctive Blue Ensign of the Fishery Protection squadron flapped lazily.

More or less aided by a couple of deckhands, a young, fair-haired figure in overalls and an ancient, dirtied shirt was struggling with one of the clumsy hose-booms. As Carrick arrived, a wave larger than the rest broke against *Marlin*'s side. She rolled, a light curtain of spray drenched across her stern – and the boom clattered loose with a swinging, drunken suddenness which almost swept both deckhands over the side.

Springing forward, Carrick helped the trio secure it again.

'Look . . .' The fair-haired youngster pointed helplessly while the deckhands stood back. 'Look at it, Webb – who'll tell the Old Man?'

The hose-boom's swivel mounting had cracked across the metal. Carrick sighed and shook his head. Jumbo Wills, *Marlin*'s second mate, owed his nickname to his build and, like now, to an unhappy genius for stumbling into trouble.

'It wasn't my fault,' declared Wills indignantly, flushing under the deckhands' grins.

'No.' Carrick fought down a chuckle of his own. 'But other people might not see it that way. Leave it – I'll get something rigged to hold it for a spell. And watch how you handle the other one.' He glanced at the deckhands. 'Move. You've had a long enough rest.'

4

Leaving them, Carrick headed for the shelter of the open stern companionway and made his way along to the scuba gear storeroom. As usual, the door was hooked open. Inside, sprawled back in comfort on a couple of equipment boxes, a bull-like figure looked up, nodded a greeting, and swung to his feet, all without disturbing the long ash on the cigarette dangling from his lips.

'Like a mug o' coffee, sir?' Petty Officer William 'Clapper' Bell, their bo'sun, thumbed towards the pot steaming gently on a hot-plate in one corner. Ex-Royal Navy, six feet of solid, muscular Glasgow-Irishman, Clapper Bell used the tiny scuba room as his unofficial headquarters. 'I was thinkin' about having some.'

'It can keep,' said Carrick dryly. 'Jumbo Wills needs some help.'

'Again?' Bell scratched his close-cropped red hair, his rugged face twisting in a grin. 'What's it this time? If he's set fire to the paint store again . . .'

'No.' That had been a famous occasion. 'One of the detergent booms has come unstuck.'

'Those things?' The bo'sun grimaced, dropped his cigarette on the deck, and stamped a foot on it. 'All right, I'll take a look. But one of those days the Old Man will drown our Mr Wills in a bucket – an' I'll bring the water.'

'You'll get in the queue,' said Carrick dryly. Neither of them worried much about formal discipline when they were alone. Together they formed *Marlin*'s underwater diving team when needed and that kind of partnership developed its own personal code. 'Another thing, Clapper. Send two men to the bridge – look-out duty. We're trying to find an oil-slick.'

'I hadn't heard we'd flamin' lost one,' said Bell gloomily. Starting for the door, he thumbed again at the coffee-pot on the way. 'Help yourself.'

Carrick found a mug and did, then perched himself on the compressor unit they used to recharge the aqualung cylinders. Sipping the coffee, he grimaced. Nobody liked the hose-booms or the stack of detergent drums piled below. But somebody had to do the job. Tug-owners needed only one experience of what an oil-dispersing detergent could do to decks and paintwork then fought shy of getting involved again.

So it had been handed to Fishery Protection. Webb Carrick grimaced down at the brass-buttoned naval uniform he wore over a thick white roll-necked sweater. He'd be in overalls for that caper. Overalls made him think of Jumbo Wills again and the grimace faded, his broad-boned face splitting in a brief grin which suddenly made him look considerably younger than his thirty-one years.

A stocky five-foot-ten in height, skin weather-bronzed and dark brown hair cut short, Carrick carried most things with an easy-going if slightly sardonic humour. Most, but not all. A strong nose and dark brown eyes gave additional strength to lips which were a little too thin and which could offer a warning.

Even Captain Shannon had learned there were times when his chief officer could be pushed too far.

Gulping more of the coffee, Carrick glanced out of the storeroom's porthole. He'd been away from the bridge longer than he'd thought and the little island that had previously been on the horizon was now drawing near on the starboard bow. Its name on the charts was Moorach Island. What it amounted to was an ugly chunk of cliffs and rock, topped by grass, inhabited only by seabirds and seals.

Far behind it was another faint smudge of land. That was the sprawling island of Skye, mountains

6

reaching up to the clouds, townships usually bustling with tourist traffic from the mainland. There'd be hell to pay if an oil-slick reached those beaches.

Setting down the mug, he headed back towards the bridge. Halfway there he stopped, frowning, as *Marlin*'s engine beat took a sudden drop in revolutions and the deck lurched under an equally sudden turn to starboard.

Carrick covered the rest of the distance in a hurry.

When he got there, *Marlin* was creeping in towards Moorach Island with speed down to little more than steerage way. Captain Shannon had quit the command chair and was over at the starboard bridge wing, beside one of the recently arrived look-outs. Both had glasses focussed on the shore ahead.

Hearing Carrick arrive, Shannon lowered his glasses.

'Take a look,' he invited curtly, passing them over.

Carrick used the glasses and winced. Stranded by the receding tide and lying half-over on her side, a fishing boat was jammed against a jagged ridge of rock. Planking had been ripped open below the waterline near her bow. She had part of a torn net still trailing in the sea which lapped against her exposed stern. But there was no sign of life aboard.

Shannon crossed over and jabbed the siren button. *Marlin* bellowed a long, inquiring blast, then another as he pressed again.

Carrick saw a seal make a panic-stricken dive from a ledge and the splash as it hit the sea. Gulls and terns rose by the score from their nests along the cliffs and circled angrily. But no one answered from the boat or appeared along the desolate shore.

'Take the Z-boat,' said Shannon soberly. 'Check her over, mister.'

* * *

Carrick took two men with him, Clapper Bell and a lanky East Coast deckhand named Harry Roberts. The Z-boat, a rubber inflatable with a powerful outboard motor, foamed on her way as soon as the Fishery cruiser had anchored. But as they came nearer the island Carrick had to throttle back to thread through the scatter of low-tide rocks which guarded the shore.

'She'll drift the rest,' called Clapper Bell at last, perched watchfully at the bow.

Cutting the engine, Carrick swung the propeller clear. Moments later the Z-boat nudged its way past a barely submerged reef, then, lifted by a breaking wave, touched the pebbled beach. They dragged the boat high and dry and Roberts secured the bow-line to a rock while Carrick and the bo'sun looked around.

They'd landed about fifty yards from the fishing boat, separated from her by a tangle of rock and sea-weed. A fifty-foot seine-netter, she had the name *Harvest Lass* painted on her bow in faded gold lettering. Where the planking had been ripped, the interior of her fo'c'sle was exposed – a confused litter, including mattresses and bedding. The rest of the boat seemed relatively intact, but the deck area was still hidden by the angle at which she lay.

'I'd hate like hell to have to refloat her out o' there,' mused Bell with a professional interest. 'Even after that hole's patched it's goin' to be a job to get her clear.'

'That's somebody else's worry,' said Carrick neutrally, collecting the lightweight radio he'd brought along and slinging its strap over one shoulder. 'You and I will check the boat. Roberts, you take a prowl along the shore.'

Clapper Bell at his heels, he set off over the slippery weed and rocks. Reaching the stranded hull, they

8

scrambled round towards her bow, then had their first clear view of the deck.

'God Almighty,' said Bell with a startled intake of breath.

For a moment Carrick stayed where he was, just staring.

The *Harvest Lass* had a motionless figure sprawled over her midships winch gear. His bald head was pressed oddly against the metal and he was dressed in an old blue work-jacket, serge trousers and heavy seaboots. Ropes still led over the side from the winch to the tattered fragments of net and the fish hatch lay open, awaiting a catch that would never come.

Pulling themselves up, they quickly crossed the slanting, already bone-dry deck and reached the dead man. He'd been middle-aged, with a small, dark moustache and light blue eyes which stared lifelessly from a tanned, thin face still twisted in a final horror.

The rest was easy enough to understand. Both ends of a grey woollen scarf were trapped in the winch, which was still in gear. When the scarf had been pulled in it had tightened round the fisherman's neck, dragging him down, strangling him before he could escape.

There were scratches on his neck where he'd tried to claw the scarf loose. One hand still lay outstretched in a final, desperate effort to reach the winch controls. But the winch had tightened on until it finally jammed.

'Poor basket,' muttered Bell. 'If he was alone . . .'

Carrick nodded, then headed for the wheelhouse. It was in tumbled disorder, but the big gear lever was still engaged, the engine throttle set at slow and the small, well-worn steering wheel had been tied with a piece of light line. He could imagine the rest. The

Harvest Lass sailing on, only a dead man aboard, till she'd reached Moorach Island and had blindly smashed ashore.

Clapper Bell had gone down into the tiny fo'c'sle. He could see Roberts still working his way along the shore, though that was probably a waste of time now. Searching the wheelhouse, Carrick found a tattered logbook buried under some other papers. As he turned with it in his hands he bumped against an opened haversack hanging from a hook. It had a coffee flask and a package of sandwiches stowed inside.

Nobody would use them now. Going out on deck he saw *Marlin* had swung bow-on to the island, held by her anchor in a safe six fathoms of water. A faint shimmer of exhaust was coming from her squat stack and he knew Captain Shannon would be prowling impatiently on the bridge, waiting.

Shrugging slightly, he went back to the winch and looked down grimly at the dead man. There were better ways to die.

A couple of minutes passed before Clapper Bell padded back along the deck to join him. The burly bo'sun shook his head at the unspoken question.

'Looks like he was on his own, sir. Though she's pretty big for one man to handle an' fish.'

Carrick nodded. Normally a boat like the *Harvest Lass* would operate with a crew of three aboard. But one experienced man could sail her at a pinch – provided nothing went wrong.

'Got your knife?' he asked.

Silently, Bell handed over the cork-handled diving knife he always carried sheathed at his belt. Carefully Carrick used the sharp steel and cut through the taut wool of the scarf. As the last strands parted the dead

10

man's body shifted slightly then, limbs still locked in a crab-like rigour, slid slowly to the deck.

Tight-lipped, ignoring the staring blue eyes, Carrick bent down, opened the work-jacket, and found a leather wallet in the inside pocket. It held some pound notes, a few creased papers and a driving licence.

'John MacBean, Harbour View Cottages, Portcoig, Skye.' He showed Bell the licence details, then returned it to the wallet.

'So he's not far from home,' commented Bell dryly.

Carrick didn't answer for a moment. Portcoig was a fishing village on the south-west coast of Skye, maybe fifteen miles away. *Marlin* had been there a few months back and he'd spent a night drinking with Dave Rother, who made Portcoig his shark-catching base.

He thought for a moment of Rother, probably still chasing that basking shark a few miles away. Rother was the type who made as many enemies as friends for a wide variety of reasons. But he would know MacBean. In a place the size of Portcoig everyone knew everybody.

'The Old Man will be wonderin' what's going on,' mused Clapper Bell significantly.

'I'll call him.' Carrick grimaced slightly at the thought. 'Tell Roberts he can stop beach-combing.' His eyes strayed to the dead man again. 'Then get a blanket, Clapper. Cover him up.'

He turned away, dragged out the little radio, switched on, and pulled out the built-in aerial. *Marlin*'s duty operator answered immediately when he called. Then, after a brief pause, Shannon's voice came through in a crackling roar. *Marlin*'s captain had a firm belief that microphones only behaved when the user was shouting.

'Well, mister? You took long enough. Over.'

11

Carrick gave him a quick, factual rundown on the situation, then waited, the murmur of the sea a background to the soft crackle of static from the hand-set.

'Right.' Shannon came back again. 'Care to guess when it happened?'

'Probably during the night, sir.' Carrick had a hazy recollection that a body usually began stiffening after ten or twelve hours. 'It looks that way.'

'I'll ask the coastguards to check with Portcoig that the damned fool did go out on his own,' said Shannon brusquely. 'But meantime we'll take him aboard. Don't worry about his boat – nobody's going to sail her anywhere for a spell. Out, mister.'

The static took over again.

As soon as Roberts had joined them they made a crude stretcher from a grating, loaded the dead man on to it, then made the difficult journey back over the rocks to the Z-boat. The blanket-covered shape lying at the bow, they got the outboard motor going, and headed back across the water towards the waiting Fishery cruiser.

They were almost there, near enough to identify the crewmen waiting in a little group just below the bridge, when Roberts gave a mutter of surprise and pointed further out.

'Look, sir.'

Carrick looked in the direction the deckhand indicated. The small, dark shape of another fishing boat was plugging towards Moorach Island at a steady pace. The silhouette of the harpoon gun at the bow made her easy enough to identify. Dave Rother and his *Seapearl* were going to be with them in a matter of minutes.

'Now there's a coincidence,' muttered Clapper Bell with an unusual edge.

'He probably tuned to the Fishery Protection frequency, heard some of the talk, and got interested,' answered Carrick. Plenty of boats did the same when a Protection cruiser was around. He glanced again at the approaching shark-catcher, then concentrated on bringing the Z-boat round in a slow curve which would bring her alongside *Marlin*. 'We'll find out soon enough. Anyway, they're from the same village.'

'But Rother's a sharkman,' grunted Bell.

'Meaning?'

The bo'sun shook his head and didn't elaborate. As they eased in beside the Fishery cruiser's hull, Roberts tossed a line to the men above. It was secured, they worked their way along to a lowered ladder, and Carrick clambered up. Reaching the deck, he almost collided with a thin, sour-faced figure.

'What's the rush?' demanded Pettigrew, *Marlin*'s junior second mate.

Carrick took it with a smile. He made allowances for Pettigrew most of the time. It made life easier. By far the oldest of the ship's three watchkeeping officers even though he ranked as junior, Pettigrew was a surly character in his fifties who had come back to sea for reasons he kept to himself. When he wasn't on watch he spent most of his time in his cabin, sleeping or reading.

'I missed your friendly face,' said Carrick cheerfully. 'Any more word from the coastguards?'

'Who'd tell me?' shrugged Pettigrew. He looked down at the Z-boat with distaste. 'Well, at least we're not chasing after that oil-slick. I'll take over here. The Old Man wants you.'

13

Carrick headed for the bridge. Captain Shannon greeted him with a nod then thumbed in the direction of the approaching *Seapearl*.

'Seen him?'

'Yes, sir.'

Shannon shrugged. 'Well, he's your friend, not mine. I've heard too many stories about how he operates. You can talk to him.' The bearded moon-face scowled a little. 'Then we'll head for Portcoig and land that fisherman. Your guess was right, mister. The damned fool sailed from there late last night alone, and with his gut awash in beer. The coastguard say he'd some kind of problem gathering his usual crew.'

Carrick nodded his understanding and saw Jumbo Wills' overalled figure heading along the deck towards the bow.

'What about that oil-slick, sir?'

'If there was one, it must have broken up. Department say they've spoken to two lobster boats who should have been right in the middle of it – we've to forget about the thing meantime. Which should relieve some people.'

'Sir?' Carrick could almost sense it coming.

'Mister, I've seen that broken spray-boom,' said Shannon softly. 'A captain is supposed to know what's going on aboard his ship. If we'd found that slick what were we supposed to do? Try scooping it up with damned soup spoons?' He snorted, a glint of icy warning in his eyes. 'Well, I've already dealt with that young fool Wills, and this time I'll leave it at that. But it doesn't happen again. Understood?'

Carrick nodded, wondering how badly Jumbo Wills had been blistered. 'I'm having the boom fixed, sir.'

'Between you, you'd better,' said Shannon bleakly, turning away and reaching for the bridge intercom

14

phone. 'Don't waste time over that damned shark-man, either. They'll be waiting for us at Portcoig.

Nobody could have described the *Seapearl* as beautiful. Her original lines had been hacked away to allow for the harpoon gun's platform, the wheelhouse was a strange, elevated structure, and the big deckhouse added aft looked like the work of a do-it-yourself weekend – which it had been. As she stopped and rolled gently in the swell within hailing distance of the Fishery cruiser, her dark, paint-blistered hull showed green with weed along the waterline.

There were crewmen on her deck. But the hail from the shark-catcher came from a lean, fair-haired man in khaki shirt and slacks who emerged from the tall, platform-like wheelhouse.

'Ahoy, *Marlin*,' – he bellowed across the gap, not bothering about any kind of megaphone – 'anything we can do?'

'About what, Dave?' Out on the bridge wing, Carrick saved his lungpower and used a battery loud-hailer.

Dave Rother stared then waved a greeting. 'Come off it, Webb. That Portcoig boat all the fuss is on about. Can we help?'

'No. Only one man aboard, dead. Somebody called John MacBean,' answered Carrick. 'Know him?'

The metallic echo of the loud-hailer faded and for a long moment there was no reply.

'I know him,' shouted Rother at last. 'What happened?'

An impatient rumble came from Shannon in the command chair. Carrick looked round, nodded, and raised the loud-hailer again.

15

'Tell you when you get back to Portcoig. Where's that shark you were chasing?'

'Lost it,' answered Rother ruefully. 'You know the story – there's no luck fishing with a woman aboard.'

Carrick blinked, forgot Shannon's impatience and demanded, 'What woman?'

'The new nurse at Portcoig. Showing her how sharkers live.' He turned, said something, and a girl emerged from the wheelhouse. She was tall, slim and a redhead, wearing a white sweater and black trousers. Rother cupped his hands again. 'We chased here in case she could help. But if he's dead and we can't – well, that's that. See you later.'

Rother took the girl's arm and they went back into the wheelhouse. A moment later the shark-catcher's propeller began to churn and she swung away, engine thudding.

Carrick laid down the loud-hailer and looked round. The helmsman was stony-faced but had a twinkle in his eyes. Shannon showed a thundercloud impatience.

'If you're finished, mister, we'll get back to work,' he said curtly, reaching for the intercom phone.

Taking his chance, the helmsman caught Carrick's eye and winked.

Once under way, *Marlin* swung on a north-easterly course for Portcoig. Her twin 2,000-horsepower diesels gulping air with a steady roar, she built up speed and the white wash gradually thickened at her square-cut stern.

A routine weather report reached the bridge from the radio room. Conditions would be unchanged for the next twenty-four hours. The helmsman was relieved, Captain Shannon disappeared to his day-

16

cabin, and soon afterwards Pettigrew arrived to take over the watch. Carrick handed over then went below to the little wardroom aft. The steward was working in his shirt-sleeves, cleaning up, but he had some coffee warming in the galley and brought a filled mug.

Carrick took the mug along to his cabin, peeled off his uniform jacket, kicked out of his thick-soled seaboots, then sprawled back on his bunk with the coffee in one hand and a cigarette in the other.

They would be at Portcoig in about an hour. By the time the dead fisherman had been taken ashore and the inevitable formalities and reports completed he'd a feeling *Marlin* would stay there at least overnight.

Though, like everything else, that all depended on Captain Shannon. Shannon was rated as a super-intendent of fisheries, which made him answerable only to the Department's top brass. Shannon had spent a lifetime in Fishery Protection, and fairly soon would be compulsorily retired with a Civil Service pension and maybe a medal buried deep in the small print of some Honours List.

But until that happened his powers were impres-sive, his task that of keeping the peace and main-taining the law in the multi-million-pound Scottish fishing industry – an industry where life could be dangerously harsh and tempers often flared violently. There was a multiplicity of rules and regulations to enforce, covering everything from nets and gear to seasonal bans and operating lights. There were terri-torial boundaries to enforce, with fishing craft from a dozen European nations sniffing around the fringe all the way from small Dutch herring boats to big electronics-crammed Russian trawlers.

And the fisherman you arrested one day could be the same man you tried to save from drowning the

17

next. Carrick grinned slightly at the thought. That had happened more than once. And having saved the man, they'd more than once had to arrest him again.

Most things came *Marlin*'s way, Like the rest of the Protection flotilla, she logged an average of 17,000 sea miles a year on her West Coast beat.

A lot of that distance meant the Hebridean chain: five hundred islands, from uninhabited pimples of rock onward, scattered in a great 130-mile off-shore chain. People romanced about the Hebrides. To the watchdog Fishery cruisers they meant dangerous shoals, treacherous, narrow channels and giant tidal rips, all exposed to the worst of Atlantic weather.

While the average fisherman and islander used the term 'Fishery snoop' as close to a curse and regarded a Fishery cruiser as a form of grey-painted plague.

But *Marlin* and her kind still patrolled regardless. She had no deck guns. Her authority was her thirty-knot speed, her Blue Ensign with the Fishery crest, and, above all, Shannon, with his right to be prosecutor, judge and jury when the occasion demanded.

Yawning, Carrick finished the last of the coffee, took another long draw on his cigarette, stubbed it out, and was thinking again about the dead fisherman when there was a knock at the cabin door. It opened and Clapper Bell looked round.

'Got a moment, sir?' asked the bo'sun cheerfully.

'Yes.' Carrick eyed the big Glasgow-Irishman with a suspicion born of experience. Bell came in, closed the door, and beamed at him.

'The word is we'll be staying overnight at Portcoig, sir,' began Bell. He rubbed a massive paw of a hand warily along his chin. 'At least, so I've heard . . .'

'From a reliable source.' Carrick finished it for him. 'Don't ask me, Clapper. I don't know.'

'We will,' said Bell confidently. 'The Old Man told Cookie to draw up a galley stores list. And he asked the engine room how much fuel the tanks could take.'

Carrick sighed. 'So?'

'So probably we'll be goin' ashore tonight.' Bell eyed him innocently. 'Except that I've hardly the price o' a decent drink till next pay-day. And – uh . . .'

'And there's a barmaid at Portcoig with starving children to support,' said Carrick wearily. He swung himself up from the bunk, reached for his jacket, and found his wallet. 'How much?'

'Two quid – uh . . .' Bell grinned, palmed the notes and began to ease back towards the door. 'Thanks.'

'Hold on.' Carrick beckoned him back. 'Now it's your turn. You mumbled something about Dave Rother being a sharkman. I've had the same thing from the Old Man, but they just don't get on, never have. Rother pulled a fast one on him years ago. But what about you?'

Bell shrugged, the grin fading into a reluctant frown. 'He's a pal o' yours.'

'We've had a few drinks together,' corrected Carrick. 'Let's have it.'

'I thought you'd know.' Bell sucked his teeth unhappily. '*Skua*'s bo'sun told me what happened.'

Carrick raised an eyebrow. *Skua* was their sister ship; they'd relieved her at the start of the patrol.

'Go on.'

'Well, Rother's base is at Portcoig, right? An' his boys used to get on fine wi' the locals . . .'

'Used to?'

Bell nodded. 'Not any more they don't. There's the next best thing to open bloody war goin' on now. The locals want the sharkmen out. In fact, they tried to burn them out so I was told. An' Rother's played rough too.'

19

'Why?'

'I don't know, sir.' Bell grimaced. 'But,' – he glanced down at his hand – 'well, I'll bet you this two quid we soon find out.'

Carrick quickly shook his head. *Marlin*'s bo'sun seldom took chances where money was concerned.

Chapter Two

Marlin reached Skye and the mile-wide curve of Camsha Bay at 4 p.m., her speed coming down to a four-knot crawl as she came through the buoyed entrance channel that led to Portcoig.

'It all looks peaceful enough,' said Jumbo Wills hopefully. He was leaning beside Carrick on the boat-deck rail, still in overalls, ready to disappear again at the first sign of Shannon. 'But if Clapper is right . . .'

'He's always right,' said Carrick resignedly. 'That's why I told him to pass the word around the crew. Then they can at least try to keep out of trouble ashore.'

Silently, they watched the Fishery cruiser's slow, curving approach towards Portcoig. The tiny harbour made an ideal base for small craft. Even the shoal rocks which lurked outside played their part in offering shelter from the Atlantic and once inside the bay there was a gentle, grassy foreshore where sheep were grazing.

Beyond that, heather-clad slopes began a rapid rise towards the shadowed, jagged peaks of the Cuillin hills. There were no trees. Instead, a line of sun-bleached telephone poles followed the narrow, single-track road which snaked into the hills from Portcoig's scatter of houses.

Carrick glanced round. Half a mile across the bay was Camsha Island, where Dave Rother had his shark-catching base. A low-lying blob of land, separated from the north shore by a stretch of tidal sand and shingle, people could walk out to it from the other side of the bay when the tide was right. Maybe base was too impressive a description. It amounted to a long concrete slipway and a collection of huts, the largest hut a processing factory and the others used as living quarters for his men or to hold supplies for the three boats he operated.

'Webb.' Jumbo Wills nudged him and nodded towards Portcoig pier, a long, stone structure ending in a T-shaped wooden head. Several small seine-net boats were tied along it and a group of men were waiting near the end. 'We've got a welcoming committee.'

'Including the local law.' One of the men wore police uniform. Then he smiled slightly, spotting a small red and white motor-launch which had rounded the pier with a solitary figure in its open cockpit. 'There's something that hasn't changed. Aunt Maggie is still in business.'

Coming in smartly, the little launch slipped neatly between two of the fishing boats and tied up. Most people who came to Portcoig met Maggie MacKenzie. A widow, she wasn't young any more and nobody knew who'd first given her the nickname Aunt Maggie. But it fitted. She and her boat constituted the ferry service which linked Portcoig with half a dozen little crofting communities scattered around the local coast.

That could mean carrying children to school, sheep to market or tourists round the bay – anything, in fact, that needed a boat for hire.

22

'I'd call her indestructible,' mused Wills. 'She even had a glint in her eye about Pettigrew last trip.'

'Once she discovered he wasn't married – and on the Old Man before that, till she discovered he was,' grinned Carrick. The grin faded as he remembered why they'd come. 'Better get to that bow-line – unless you want another roasting.'

The Fishery cruiser was still slowly, barely moving as she edged in towards a vacant berth. Wills didn't need a second telling. Nodding, he started off at a trot.

Three of the reception committee came aboard as soon as *Marlin's* gangway was positioned. Led by the police officer, two sober-faced men in Sunday-best suits came across it and were met by Captain Shannon. One of the men had a black tie in mourning and Shannon took all three straight to his day-cabin.

After a spell they reappeared and went aft to the deck-house being used as a temporary mortuary. When they returned to the day-cabin Carrick was summoned to join them.

When he entered he found Shannon and his visitors seated round the table in the small, sparsely furnished cabin. A bottle of Shannon's prized single-malt whisky was on the table and each man had a filled glass.

'My chief officer,' said Shannon shortly. 'He found the body.'

'And cut the scarf?' The police officer, a sergeant, nursed his whisky glass with a frown shaping on his beefy face.

'Would you expect him to bring the blasted winch back?' asked Shannon icily. He glanced at Carrick. 'This is Sergeant Fraser from Carbost, the nearest police station. Then Alec MacBean, the dead man's brother' – the man in the black tie, thin and middle-aged, nodded – 'and Harry Graham, who was half-owner with John MacBean of the *Harvest Lass*.'

Graham, a tall man, grey-haired and the oldest of the trio, cleared his throat. 'We hear the boat is badly damaged. Eh . . . how bad?' He blinked quickly at his companions. 'It can wait, of course. But I might as well know now.'

'She can be salvaged but it won't be easy,' said Carrick, and saw him wince. 'She's badly ripped below the waterline and after you get her off it will still be a repair-yard job.'

'I'm more interested in what happened to John,' muttered Alec MacBean. 'I've that right – I'm his only relative.' He scowled. 'What kind o' an accident is it when a man gets strangled in his own winch?'

'Not unique,' said Shannon neutrally. 'I've heard of it happening.' He glanced from Carrick to the bottle. 'You'll find a spare glass in the locker, mister.'

Carrick nodded his thanks, found the glass, and poured himself a drink. He sipped it neat. There was no water on the table and Shannon would have regarded the suggestion as an insult to his single-malt.

'I still wish you hadn't need to cut the scarf,' sighed Sergeant Fraser. 'You know how it is, Chief Officer. There'll be a fatal-accident inquiry, before a jury.'

'At which he'll give evidence,' snapped Shannon impatiently. 'Trying to stir up a murder case, Sergeant?'

Fraser flushed. 'Captain, I'm not looking for work. I wouldn't be here if Carbost wasn't the only police station within miles of this place. And as for having to drive over that damned goat-track of a road to get here . . .'

'You'll have two witnesses, Sergeant,' soothed Carrick. 'Our bo'sun was with me. The only thing

24

that puzzled us was why the man was alone aboard.'
He glanced at Harry Graham. 'How often did that
happen?'

'I wouldn't know.' Graham shook his head and
frowned. 'I'm no fisherman, Chief Officer. I'm manager at the Broomfire Distillery up the glen.' He
glanced at MacBean. 'Alec can tell you my share in the
Harvest Lass is just money invested.'

Carrick considered the grey-haired man with a new
interest. Whisky was Portcoig's other industry and its
Broomfire distillery was justly famed. There were
plenty of similar distilleries scattered around the
islands, most of them outposts of mainland whisky
empires – money-making outposts prized for the
uniquely individual quality of their bottled glory.

The Portcoig operation was only a few years old,
but Broomfire Supreme was already established as a
single-malt connoisseur's delight. He'd been told it
often enough by Shannon. Most of it went for export
and that, in the opinion of *Marlin*'s commander, was
an unmitigated disgrace. Broomfire was too good for
uneducated foreign palates.

He put the thought aside and tried again. 'But John
MacBean would usually have a regular crew, correct?'

'Two men at least,' nodded Graham.

'And should have had last night,' grated Alec
MacBean. His eyes, blue like the dead man's, glittered
angrily. 'Fergie Lucas and Peter Stewart should have
been with him and you can blame that damned sharkman Rother and his people that they weren't.' He
leaned forward. 'If anyone killed John it was those
sharkers – that's how the village will remember it.'

'Meaning they stopped his crew getting aboard?'
Carrick raised a surprised eyebrow.

'No,' murmured Sergeant Fraser. He finished his
whisky with a long, practised swallow, carefully ran a

finger along his lips and glanced at Shannon. 'But on the other hand, yes. There was a brawl outside the Harbour Arms at closing time last night. We had a patrol car over – as we've had most nights lately. My lads arrived in time to see Lucas and Stewart having their heads knocked against a wall by some of Rother's sharkmen.' He smiled slightly. 'They were in no state to go anywhere.'

'And how many o' Rother's men were arrested?' snapped Alec MacBean. 'Not a damned one!'

Sergeant Fraser shrugged. 'They scattered. Anyway, I've heard different stories how it started.'

'It started when Rother's men attacked them,' said MacBean harshly. 'Or are you on Rother's side, Sergeant?'

Fraser's face froze, then he rose ponderously to his feet. 'I'll forget I heard that,' he said softly. 'Captain, my thanks for your hospitality. We'll have the body taken ashore. Maybe later Chief Officer Carrick will let me have a written statement.'

Shannon nodded. Pushing back their chairs, Graham and MacBean muttered their own thanks and the trio went out, the policeman last, stopping briefly in the cabin doorway to give a slight, apologetic shrug.

As the cabin door closed again Shannon sighed, got up, and crossed over to the brass-rimmed porthole. The porthole glass was partly obscured by a large, aggressive-looking tomato plant. The plant had been a gift from his wife a few patrols back and somehow it lived and flourished on a diet which was mainly cold tea and tobacco ash.

'It might be an idea to base ourselves on Portcoig for a couple of days, mister,' he mused, parting the foliage and looked out towards Camsha Island. 'When *Skua* was here last there was trouble brewing.'

'I heard, sir.'

'Did you?' Shannon grunted under his breath, found his cigarettes, and offered one to Carrick. They shared a light from a kitchen match Shannon struck with his thumbnail.

'Ever been to an island funeral, mister?' asked Shannon unexpectedly.

Carrick shook his head.

'It's an experience.' Shannon brooded for a moment. 'I remember one that ended up like World War Three. Have you heard what started this trouble?'

'No, sir.'

'*Skua*'s captain heard a hazy story about one of Rother's men and a local girl – that she became pregnant and drowned herself off the end of the pier.' Shannon sniffed sceptically. 'I didn't think the average female worried about that sort of thing any more. Still, you could maybe have a talk with Rother and find out more about it.'

'I'll try him.' Carrick finished his drink.

'Good.' Shannon considered the empty glass briefly, then deliberately corked the whisky bottle and put it back in his locker. 'I'll probably stay aboard – I've a load of damned Department forms to catch up on. But usual shore leave tonight as far as the crew are concerned. Just tell them to keep their noses clean for once.'

An old-fashioned black motor hearse was backed up facing the gangway when Carrick went out on deck. The rear doors were open, waiting, and a mutter of voices was coming from further aft.

A moment later Pettigrew appeared. Behind him, aided by a couple of seamen, a black-coated under-taker and his assistant came into sight carrying a plain wooden coffin. They struggled up over the gangway with their burden and loaded it into the hearse. The rear doors closed. With a nod of thanks the two men went round, climbed into their seats, and the hearse purred off along the deserted pier.

Pettigrew came back aboard with an expression of relief on his thin face.

'They didn't waste any time,' said Carrick dryly.

'No.' Pettigrew looked at the little slip of white he held in one hand. 'One of those characters gave me his card. What the hell am I supposed to do with it?'

'Keep it. Maybe they give trading stamps for introductions,' said Carrick mildly.

Pettigrew glared at him. 'Very funny. When do we sail?'

'We don't.' Carrick shook his head. 'Not before morning anyway.' He looked past Pettigrew, eyes narrowing slightly. A small convoy of boats was coming through the channel into the bay. Dave Rother's shark-catching team were returning home. 'I'm going ashore for a spell. You and Jumbo toss to settle who minds the shop.'

He left Pettigrew grumbling, crossed the gangway, and headed towards the village. The main street was smooth tarmac, but the lanes leading off it were either pebbled or surfaced in rough slabs. Most of the houses were small and stone-built, with lace curtains at their narrow windows. Some had fishing nets draped across ropes in their small gardens, a few had hopeful TV aerials lashed to their squat chimneys.

'Stinking snoop!'

The shout, in a boyish treble, came from a lane. He turned in time to see a fair-haired youngster scurry round a corner and heard a cackle of laughter from a grizzled old fisherman who'd been working on a net.

28

Grinning wryly, Carrick walked on. There were few people around and the ones he passed either ignored him or nodded a brief greeting. It amounted to the average fishing village reaction to Fishery Protection uniform.

He'd started off with no particular intention. But curiosity guided him towards Harbour View Cottages, where John MacBean had lived. When he found them they were just another row of small stone houses. Most of the front-room windows had blinds drawn shut, island tradition when there was a death among neighbours.

Suddenly, a voice hailed, then Sergeant Fraser came from one of the doorways and crossed towards him.

'Looking for me, Chief Officer?'

Carrick shook his head. 'Just walking.'

'Aye.' Fraser nodded his understanding. 'John MacBean had the middle one in the row – that one with the green door. I came to have a word with his neighbours.'

'For your report.'

'Reports make the world go round,' said Fraser dryly. A faint smile creased his heavy face. 'You know that too, I imagine. Still, I'm finished here. The next thing's the post-mortem over at Broadford Hospital then the inquiry is pretty well wrapped up as far as I'm concerned.'

'Other people may think differently,' mused Carrick.

'If you mean we may have trouble tonight . . .' The policeman didn't finish, but nodded. 'We'll have a patrol car over again, just in case.' He glanced at his watch. 'It's time I got back to Carbost. My car is at the harbour if you're heading that way again.'

Carrick nodded and they started back the way he'd come. The dull cloud overhead was thickening, with a hint of rain in the air, and they walked silently for a few moments.

'Sergeant, we've our own interest in this,' he said quietly. 'What's the story you've heard about this feud with Rother's people?'

'Feud?' Fraser slowed and scratched his chin. 'That's maybe a strong word, Chief Officer. A few brawls, a middling-sized fire that was probably just an accident . . .'

'And a patrol car you send over most nights,' finished Carrick bluntly. 'There was a girl in it, right?'

'Aye.' The policeman nodded a greeting to a passing figure. 'So they say, anyway. Her name was Helen Grant. She . . . well, she went for a late-night stroll along the pier about three months back. They found her drowned the next morning.' He shrugged. 'Accidental death – she couldn't swim, must have fallen over the edge.'

They were nearly back at the harbour. Sergeant Fraser stopped beside a small black Ford station wagon and opened the door.

'I heard she was pregnant,' said Carrick quietly. 'Who was the man?'

'Don't ask me,' said Fraser gruffly. 'For a start, she wasn't local – just a student lassie from Glasgow who came visiting to Portcoig a few times. But she had a family back in Glasgow. It was bad enough on them losing a daughter. The way I saw things they'd only have been hurt a lot worse if we'd built it up into a suicide.' His mouth hardened. 'Accidental drowning, Chief Officer. The rest of it is between her and her Maker. Agreed?'

He got into the Ford, slammed the door shut, and started the motor. Then, suddenly, he wound down his window.

'If you want gossip, Chief Officer, there's your best bet.' Fraser thumbed out across the bay. Aunt Maggie's small red and white launch was coming in again, heading towards the harbour from Camsha Island.

The station wagon grated into gear and the policeman set it moving in an angry way that sent gravel spurting from the tyres.

By the time the ferry launch nosed in, Carrick had positioned himself near her landing stage on the pier. He watched the spry, grey-haired woman who moved quickly along the boat from the tiller to tie a bow-line round an iron ring set in one of the massive timbers, then deliberately walked nearer as the ferry's three passengers disembarked and came up the steps towards him.

Big Yogi Dunlop, the gunner from Dave Rother's *Seapearl*, was built like a barrel, had dark, shaggy hair, and dwarfed the girl by his side. She was the redhead who had appeared from the shark-catcher's wheelhouse. Trailing a yard or so behind, their companion was a tall, thin youngster in an old jersey and slacks. His face badly swollen, one eye blackened and half-shut, he walked carefully as if every step hurt.

'Hello, Chief – seeing you is a bit o' luck,' boomed Dunlop happily, shoving his hands deep in the pockets of his leather jacket. 'The boss gave me a message for you. He says you can buy him a drink at the White Cockade tonight.'

'What time?' asked Carrick. There were only two bars in Portcoig and the White Cockade was the more popular.

He was looking at the girl. Seen close-up, her sweater and trousers outfit moulded a figure which might have been hand-carved for perfection. The tanned, lightly freckled face was strong on character, with calm grey eyes which were slightly amused as they met his own. She had a pert nose and a slightly dimpled chin and her copper-red hair, long and straight, was tied at the nape of the neck by a long white ribbon.

'About nine, I suppose,' answered Dunlop vaguely. 'That's his usual, right, Peter?'

The boy with the damaged face shaped a sound of sullen agreement and shuffled his feet as if anxious to get away.

'Yogi . . .' Carrick glanced significantly towards the girl.

'Hell, I forgot,' declared the gunner cheerfully. 'Sorry, Chief. This is Sheila Francis, the new district nurse here. And the lad is Peter Benson, who – uh – well, he's been workin' with us.'

'Was working with you,' said Benson in a bitter mumble. His normally thin features twisted with an effort. 'Why bother to cover up? I don't damned well care. Not now.'

Dunlop sighed sympathetically. 'You know how it is, boy. The boss gives the orders, not me.' He switched his attention back to Carrick. 'Do I tell the boss you'll be there?'

'Yes. But he can do the buying.'

'Maybe.' The gunner grinned, then beckoned to Benson. 'Come on, then. Let's get you fixed up like the boss said. An' cheer up, for God's sake. He's doin' you a favour.'

Benson scowled, but followed the big man obediently along the pier towards the village, leaving Carrick with the girl.

'Yogi wouldn't win prizes for introductions,' mused Carrick.

'I've had better,' she agreed wryly. 'But at least I know who you are. Dave talked about you.'

Carrick grinned. 'Which makes a bad start. On your day off?'

She nodded. 'Dave promised me a trip and this was it.' Her smile faded. 'It – well, it didn't turn out like I expected. We heard the radio messages. I knew John MacBean – not well, but I'd talked to him.' Glancing past him along the pier, she frowned. 'That boy with Yogi – Peter Benson. Dave said MacBean's two crewmen attacked him last night. Then there was some kind of general battle. Was that why MacBean was alone out there?'

'It seems that way.' A gull swooped down, landed near them with a quick wing-flutter, then strutted fearlessly. Carrick shrugged. 'He was a damned fool taking a boat like the *Harvest Lass* out on his own. Did Dave say what started the fight?'

A sudden caution in her grey eyes, Sheila Francis shook her head. The white hair-ribbon brushed tantalizingly along her neck.

'And now Dave has fired him.' Carrick waited, saw no response, and tried a different tack. 'Meeting Dave tonight?'

'Not a chance,' she said wryly. 'Having a day off doesn't mean too much in a place like this. I've some patients to look in on tonight.'

'And afterwards?'

She shrugged. 'Not the White Cockade. I've landed in enough hot water since I came here without looking for more. Portcoig's view of a district nurse is that she should be above wanting a drink.'

'And what does the nurse feel about it?'

Her laugh was a soft chuckle. 'I'll tell you some other time. Goodbye, Chief Officer.'

'If Rother is Dave, then I'm Webb,' he told her. 'Otherwise I call you Nurse.'

'I'll remember.' She smiled at him again, then left, strolling confidently along the pier.

Watching, Carrick gave a silent whistle of appreciation, then turned and made his way down the ferry steps towards the launch. All he could see of its owner was her trousered bottom and legs. The rest of Maggie MacKenzie was hidden under a raised engine hatch.

'Hello, Maggie,' he said mildly.

'Go away,' came her muffled voice. 'Come back in an hour, whoever you are. I won't be ready till then – there's a fuel line needs clearing.'

'I wouldn't go out on your old tub if you paid me,' said Carrick with a grin. 'Come on out of there, Maggie.'

'Eh?' She did, wriggling out smartly, an adjustable wrench clutched in one hand. 'And just what's wrong with . . . ?' As she saw him, she stopped and sighed. 'So it's you, is it?' Using her free hand she wiped her forehead and left a smudge of oil in the process. 'Come to work or watch?'

'To talk.'

'I know what that usually means,' sniffed Maggie MacKenzie. A small, neat woman, still with a reasonable figure, she was probably in her late fifties. Skin tanned dark by the weather, she considered him with a trace of annoyance. 'Could that captain of yours not have sent Mr Pettigrew? I like my men mature.'

'I'll tell him,' promised Carrick with a twinkle. 'But coming here was my own idea.'

'That's even worse.' She still looked interested. 'All right, sit down somewhere. You're too big to have standing around.'

Carrick settled in the stern thwarts. Maggie MacKenzie joined him, took the cigarette he offered, and cupped her hands round the flame of his lighter.

'When you say "talk" you mean you want to hear the local gossip,' she declared after a first puff of smoke. 'Well, what do you want to know?'

Carrick lit his own cigarette first. 'How much trouble John MacBean's death could cause.'

'A lot.' Her mouth tightened at the thought. 'No one here needs a crystal ball for that. Things have been heading from bad to worse as it is, ever since . . .'

'Ever since Helen Grant drowned?'

Her eyes narrowed. 'If you know that, why ask?'

'I'd like more of the story, Maggie. More than I could get out of Sergeant Fraser, though he practically admitted he covered up a suicide in his report.'

'For the girl's family.' The woman nodded and considered the lapping water pensively. 'Aye, as police go that man Fraser's decent enough. And what's your interest in it all? I'd have thought pregnant fish were more in your line.'

He ignored the thrust. 'Who do people say the man was, Maggie?'

She frowned and flicked ash from her cigarette. 'You never waste time, do you? Well, some say it was Dave Rother. Others say that lad I just brought over, the one that looked like he'd been hit by a truck.'

'Young Benson?'

'Him,' she agreed dryly. 'Maybe she liked mixing her men. I'd say Dave Rother was the one she really was set on, though he was older. But if Rother wasn't around then she'd settle for young Benson.'

'Then what's your guess?' he asked.

Maggie MacKenzie shook her head. 'I suppose either o' them could have rolled her in the heather. Or it could have been someone else. Even her own uncle has no real idea.'

Carrick raised an eyebrow. 'What uncle?'

'Harry Graham – the Graham who is half-owner of the *Harvest Lass*,' she said patiently. 'You met him, didn't you?'

He nodded, surprised.

'I saw him going aboard after you came in.' She rubbed a hand along the boat's painted wood. 'Mind you, before the girl began mixing with Rother's sharkers she went around with a local lad, Fergie Lucas . . . the same Fergie who would have been on the *Harvest Lass* last night if he hadn't started beating up young Benson then found himself with a lot more on his hands.'

Carrick swore softly, and she chuckled.

'What you could call a tangle, isn't it?'

'A mess,' he confessed. 'Maggie, couldn't Lucas have been the father?'

'It would have taken some doing,' she said with a dry amusement. 'Fergie Lucas was away from here for nearly six months, working on some cargo ship on the Australia run. He didn't come back to Portcoig until just weeks before she died.'

He shrugged, gave up, and thanked her.

Most of *Marlin*'s crew were already ashore. Almost the only sounds aboard were the background hum of the generators and the below-deck's rasp of music from a transistor radio; the Fishery cruiser lay quietly at her berth as the evening wore on. Overhead, the dull cloud gave way before a freshening wind and the sky became blue, streaked with cotton-wool white.

Captain Shannon stayed in his cabin. The ward-room steward took him a meal on a tray, then made

another trip with a bottle of beer. In the wardroom
Carrick found himself eating alone until Andy Shaw,
the chief engineer, arrived. Shaw was unshaven, but
was wearing a tie with his crumpled shirt, a sure sign
he was going ashore.

'Ach, there's just the one trouble,' said Shaw
gloomily, poking at his plate with a fork. 'A man getting decently drunk is one thing. But what happens
wi' that damned engine-room squad of mine? They
get straight on the High Court cocktails – and after
that they're like bloody hospital cases for a day.'

Carrick grinned sympathetically. The engine-room
squad were welcome to their choice. It amounted to a
vicious half-pint mixture of sherry, cheap wine and
cider, a mixture which could topple any ordinary man
into near oblivion. Even a seasoned drinker could be
launched into a trouble-making stupor after a few
glasses of the stuff. Yes, 'High Court' was a sardonically appropriate name.

'Next time sign on teetotallers,' suggested Carrick
between mouthfuls. 'They'd be easier to handle.'

Shaw stared at him in horror. 'An' what the hell
would a teetotaller know about engines?' he
demanded devastatingly.

That kind of argument couldn't be won. Carrick
finished his meal, collected his cap, and went on deck.
Stopping near the gangway, he lit a cigarette and
looked around. The sun was beginning to come low
on the horizon, already casting lengthening shadows
and turning the far edge of the sea to a reddish gold.
Along the pier some of the seine-netters had sailed
but new arrivals were taking their places.

He watched another boat come in and tie up. A
truck was waiting for it and the fishing boat's crew
immediately opened the deck hatch and began to

unload their catch, already cleaned, boxed, and packed around with ice.

The truck would take that ribbon of road across the island then cross by vehicle ferry to the mainland. By the next night city families would be sitting down to eat that silver harvest.

Though their fish would cost them several times more than the fisherman collected for his sweat.

That was life. Carrick grimaced, glanced at his watch, and decided it was time he headed towards the White Cockade. He lit a cigarette and went ashore.

In the guidebooks the White Cockade, Portcoig, was listed as a tourist hotel. But in practical terms that came down to a sensible recognition of the priorities – a big, horseshoe-shaped bar with some fringe tables, a tiny dining room partitioned off in one corner, and a few token bedrooms vaguely located on the upper floor. The bar door lay open when Carrick arrived, but even so he stepped into an atmosphere which seemed compounded equally from smoke, liquor fumes and noise.

Several of *Marlin*'s crew were already elbowed up along the counter and he exchanged greetings with other faces he knew – a couple of seine-net skippers from the Mallaig fleet drinking with a prosperous-looking fish buyer, a local coastguard out of uniform and a garage foreman who'd rented him a car on pre-vious trips. But the crowd thinned considerably at one side of the horseshoe and the reason was grinning in his direction from a table just beyond it.

'Over here,' hailed Dave Rother, sitting with a small group of his men. 'I'm buying, Webb.'

'It makes a change.' Carrick took a vacant seat, ordered a whisky, listened with half an ear to Rother's light-hearted banter, but noticed that the sharkmen were still being left in isolation as far as the other fishermen along the bar were concerned.

'*Slainche*.' He used the Gaelic toast absently, took a sip of the liquor, then set the glass down. 'I want to talk with you, Dave.'

'Now there's a surprise,' said Rother sardonically. He glanced at his companions. 'That's meant as a hint. I'll see you later.'

The others rose and drifted off. Lighting a cigarette, Rother settled back and waited. He wore a blue knitted-wool jacket over his shirt and slacks and his thin, long-nosed face was expressionless. The hand which held the cigarette had a deep scar running across the palm, a reminder of a time when the shark-man had held a running rope for a fraction too long.

'Your popularity rating doesn't seem what it used to be, Dave,' said Carrick quietly, nodding slightly towards the bar.

'That's true,' agreed Rother almost lazily. He ran a finger round the rim of his glass. 'Does it worry you?'

'Should it?' parried Carrick. 'You tell me.'

Rother shrugged. 'I've an idea you know already. Maybe you've heard a story.'

'I have – or some of it.'

Carrick watched the expressionless face opposite. In another time Dave Rother would probably have found his slot in life as a freebooting privateer captain. Instead, he'd been Royal Navy for a spell, a submarine service lieutenant. But he'd resigned his commission under the threat of a court of inquiry into the complete disappearance of a startling quantity of surplus Admiralty stores. Not very long afterwards he'd appeared on the West Coast and had commenced his shark-fishing operation.

It was the kind of job which needed a Dave Rother. Basking sharks were the largest fish in the North Atlantic bar none, thirty feet long and often bigger, a minimum of five tons in weight. Only the giant Pacific whale-sharks topped them for size.

Rother went after them with his little boats and harpoon guns, caught and killed them, then processed the shark liver for its precious oil, wanted by industry and drug companies. Even an economy-sized basker would yield more than a ton of liver, meaning close to £100 cash in terms of oil.

There was money in it. But it was money won the hard way. The big sharks lived on tiny plankton. Yet they died hard, and a side-swipe from their massive tails could stove in a boat's side or smash a man's ribcage to pulp. Even so, the mere sight of those big black sail-fins above the water was enough to excite any sharkman.

'All right,' said Rother wearily, misunderstanding his silence. 'You know about the girl. But don't blame me. We had a few drinks and a few laughs together, that's all.'

'You've a man named Benson.'

'A boy,' corrected Rother sharply. 'Still in his teens – and he swears he didn't touch her.'

'So?'

Rother gave a fractional shrug. 'Laddie, when I want to let off steam I head back to civilization. Up here I work. I keep my nose reasonably clean and the same goes for my men if they want to draw their pay ... booze and the odd brawl excepted.' He emptied his glass at a gulp. 'We're the outsiders, we want to keep on good terms with the locals ... though they're a difficult shower at the best of times.'

'No trouble before the girl drowned?'

'None that mattered.'

'That's what I thought,' Carrick finished his own drink, signalled a passing barmaid, and waited till she brought two fresh glasses of whisky. Paying, he leaned closer over the table as she left. 'Dave, the way MacBean was alone on that boat isn't going to help.'

'They're blaming us, yes.' Rother set his glass down angrily. 'All right, but how did that fight last night start? MacBean's men caught young Benson on his own. They were thumping sixteen different kinds of hell out of him and starting to put in the boot when some of my lads showed up.'

'I saw Benson this afternoon,' mused Carrick. 'He said you'd fired him.'

'That's right. For his own sake – and mine,' said Rother grimly. 'I didn't like doing it. Right now he's over on the island, and he stays there till he leaves. This afternoon's trip here was so he could telephone a man he knows down south who'll maybe give him a job. Even then I had to send Yogi along as a ruddy bodyguard. Otherwise someone else might have decided to take up where Lucas and his pals stopped last night.'

'But he doesn't see it that way?'

'Would you?' Rother pursed his lips. 'There have been other things. Like the fire we had on Camsha. Nearly a thousand pounds' worth of equipment lost and it was no accident. But I can't prove a damned thing.' He glared at the fishermen clustered along the bar. 'Any one of that bunch could have started it.'

'What about the girl's uncle? Any trouble from that direction?'

Rother shook his head. 'None I know about. I went to see Graham after Helen's body was found – just to say she'd been a nice kid, that sort of thing. Nobody knew then she'd been pregnant. I've seen him a couple of times since, just passing – he hasn't said

41

anything.' He grimaced slightly. 'The *Harvest Lass* may have changed that. He's going to lose money.'

'How about the MacBean brothers, then?'

'I almost liked John. As long as he had beer money he was happy.' Rother's face hardened. 'Alec Mac-Bean is someone else. He works with Graham up at the distillery as charge-hand – and he has a reputation for being a trouble-making bastard.'

'And now his brother is dead . . .' Carrick didn't finish. 'Dave, I'd like a talk with young Benson.'

'Any time. He won't leave till the end of the week.' Rother took a long drink from his glass then his mood changed as if he'd flicked a switch. 'Yogi told me you met Sheila. Like what you saw?'

'I wouldn't complain,' Carrick grinned at him. 'She's wasted on a low-living sharker.'

'There's not much dividend in it for me,' sighed Rother sadly. 'She's a girl who sets her own pace. I found that out.'

'Does she know about Helen Grant?'

Rother shrugged. 'It was all over before she came. But knowing Portcoig, she'll have been told a few times since.'

'But she hasn't mentioned it?'

'Not to me,' answered Rother curtly, then suddenly frowned past him.

Shoving through from the door and past the crush along the bar, Yogi Dunlop reached their table a moment later. The big harpoon-gunner's face was angry as he bent over Rother and murmured in his ear. Rother's eyes widened a little then he swore softly and shoved his chair back.

'Trouble?' asked Carrick. Behind them there was already a hush among the other drinkers almost as if they'd been waiting for something to happen.

The shaggy-haired gunner nodded silently and glanced at Rother.

'Nothing we can't handle on our own,' said Rother grimly. Rising, he glared at the expectant faces along the bar. He told them loudly and bitterly, 'In case any of you didn't know, some clever bastard just cut loose those dead sharks we brought in. They're drifting in the bay now – drifting over here.' His mouth tightened. 'All right, this time we get them back. Next time we don't. If they wash ashore near the harbour they can stay there till they rot . . . and this whole village is going to be nothing but stench and flies till you get rid of them on your own.'

He stalked out, Yogi Dunlop at his heels. The men along the bar stayed silent till they'd gone, then someone raised a cheer. It spread, became laughter and a thumping of glasses on the bar.

Quietly, Carrick slowly finished his drink and left. It was beginning to dusk over outside, but he could see the long, black shapes drifting here and there in the middle of the bay. One boat was already out there among them; Rother's launch was starting out from the harbour.

On its own it wasn't much more than petty spite. But he wondered what would come next.

Chapter Three

He could have gone back for another drink and been sure of finding company. Or, further along, an equal amount of light and noise was spilling from the Harbour Bar. But for once Webb Carrick felt in a solitary mood. Uneasy without completely knowing why, he walked slowly down the deserted street. The rest of Portcoig seemed already settled for the night, doors firmly closed and windows tightly curtained. A solitary motor-cycle passed him, engine puttering, its rider not sparing him a glance.

At the end of the street he reached the bay. The tide was well out and the on-shore wind was heavy with the pungent smell of seaweed. Piping and shrilling in a constant chorus, hundreds of terns and gulls were feeding among the newly exposed rocks or pattering quick-footedly between the sandy pools. Out beyond them, in the greying dusk, Rother's boats were still working off Camsha Island.

He stayed there for a moment, lighting a cigarette, then went on towards the pier. Two men were standing together at the faraway T-end and as he headed in the same direction, passing *Marlin*'s berth, a leading hand on duty at the Fishery cruiser's gangway saluted gravely.

'All quiet?' Carrick returned the salute with a faint smile.

'Yes, sir.' The man glanced enviously towards the village. 'Down here, anyway – except for those sharker characters. They went boilin' out in a hurry.'

'They would,' agreed Carrick dryly, and left him.

Clustered fishing boats were tied two and three deep along both sides of the pier, deserted, the water lapping listlessly against their hulls, mooring ropes creaking faintly. Combined with the gathering dusk, it was a scene to delight any artist. But then artists didn't have to be up in time to take those same boats out to sea at the first hint of dawn.

The two figures on the T-end had their backs to him and Carrick was almost there before he realized who they were. Then he started to turn back, but it was too late. Hearing his footsteps, they swung round. Harry Graham greeted him with a friendly nod and Alec MacBean managed a grunt of recognition.

'Come to see the circus?' asked MacBean sardonically. He thumbed over his shoulder towards the little boats working out across the bay, still recapturing the drifting shark carcasses. 'The man who did that to Rother can have a drink on me any time.'

'Rother doesn't feel that way,' said Carrick quietly.

'It's only a taste o' what he's due,' rasped MacBean, his eyes narrowing. 'You'll find that out, believe me.'

'Easy, Alec,' said Graham warily. The tall, thin distillery manager stuck his hands in the pockets of the light raincoat he was wearing and kept his voice sympathetic. 'Everybody knows how you feel, man. But we've got enough trouble. There's no sense in making more.'

MacBean didn't answer. Graham shrugged apologetically, then asked, 'Have they any notion who sent those things drifting, Chief Officer?'

'None.' Carrick drew on his cigarette and looked at Graham consideringly. Maybe, after all, it wasn't such a bad thing they'd met. 'But I've a notion there could be a few candidates around.'

'Perhaps.' Graham sucked his thin lips briefly. 'Still, we've been on the pier about an hour and we haven't seen any kind of boat coming in from the island. Have we, Alec?'

'No. Even if we had . . .' MacBean didn't bother to finish. Turning away, he looked out into the dusk again.

'Alec and his brother were fairly close,' said Graham quietly. 'There are times when a man has a right to be bitter, Carrick.'

'I want nobody making excuses for me,' grated MacBean without glancing round.

'I know, Alec.' Graham sighed a little. 'Even so, I suppose it could have happened. Someone come in from the island, I mean.' He burrowed slightly deeper into his raincoat against the light wind. 'We've been pretty busy, loading gear on a boat I've hired to go out to Moorach tomorrow. The sooner we start trying to salvage the *Harvest Lass*, the more chance we've got.'

Carrick tossed the rest of his cigarette away. The glowing stub died as it hit the water. 'Even when she's patched she won't come off easily,' he warned. 'How about insurance?'

'She's covered,' agreed the distillery manager with minimal enthusiasm. 'But did you ever hear of an insurance company that paid out full value?'

'None that stayed in business,' said Carrick dryly. 'What boat are you using?'

'The *Heather Bee*.' Graham brightened a little. 'She's big enough for the job and her skipper is a local man, Dan Elder. He knows what he's doing.'

'He should. My brother taught him.' Alec MacBean joined them again with a scowl still on his face. 'You said you'd have another world wi' him before you left, Harry.'

Graham nodded and they started back. Walking with them, Carrick followed the men to the opposite side of the pier from where *Marlin* lay and stopped at the edge. Lying below them was a blunt-bowed eighty-foot seine-netter. She was broad beamed, with a dark, varnished hull and an overall air of inbuilt strength. Some of her deck lights were on and three men were working around her fo'c'sle hatch.

'Any problems now, Skipper?' hailed Graham.

A muscular figure in a red wool shirt shook his head. 'None, Mr Graham. An' that's the last o' the gear stowed away.'

'How about you, Fergie?' demanded MacBean. 'Sure you've got all you need?'

'And more.' The stockily built man who answered was surly. He had light brown hair cropped short and an aggressive young face which wasn't improved by a broad white patch of sticking plaster above one eyebrow. 'Hell, man – we've enough junk aboard to build another damned boat from scratch.'

'The *Harvest Lass* will do,' answered Graham with a surprising curtness. 'Make another check against your list.'

The man shrugged. Beside him, the fishing boat's skipper stifled a grin and asked, 'Will you be back before we sail, Mr Graham?'

'I'll be too busy.' Graham shook his head. 'There's a coaster coming in tomorrow for a load of whisky. But I'll call you by radio before noon.' He glanced at MacBean. 'We may as well leave them to it. Coming?'

'Eh . . . no.' MacBean rubbed a hand along his jawline. 'I want a word wi' Fergie.'

47

Graham frowned. 'All right. But remember I want you at the distillery early tomorrow. We've plenty to do.'

'I'll walk back with you,' said Carrick easily. 'As far as the village, anyway.'

'Suit yourself.' Graham gestured a farewell to the men below then turned away. They started off, Carrick keeping pace with the distillery manager's long, quick stride.

'Was that Fergie Lucas down there?' asked Carrick.

'Yes.' Graham's sniff was eloquent. 'It was his damned fault as much as anyone's that the *Harvest Lass* was wrecked. So I'm giving him the job of helping get her off again ... Stewart, the other deckie, is going too.'

'Compulsory penance?'

'Partly. But they also know what they're doing.' Graham broke his step to avoid a tangle of mooring ropes. 'And it'll keep them out of the way of fresh trouble.' He flicked a sideways glance at Carrick. 'You'll find Alec MacBean an equal problem.'

'I'd heard,' agreed Carrick. 'But it sounds like you could keep him busy tomorrow. How much whisky are you shipping out?'

'Our usual quarterly quota, 20,000 gallons of matured malt in 100-gallon casks – plus a special order, another 16,000 gallons in 2,000-gallon bulk tanks.' Graham scowled in the fading light. 'All of it still at 105 degree proof, Customs sealed and under bond. That's where the real work comes in. We've to account for every damned drop at either end of the trip or the taxman is on our top.'

'It's a lot of liquor,' said Carrick appreciatively as they skirted a pile of fish boxes.

'For here, yes. But not by head office standards. Broomfire Distillery is the smallest in the company

group, though they've a habit of forgetting it.'
Graham sounded slightly bitter. 'Our single-malt is all
seven-year-old spirit, top quality. But the bulk stuff is
three-year spirit they want for blending – too young
the way I see it. Not that head office give any particular damn what I say.'

They walked on in silence until they reached the
shore end of the pier and the first cottages were just
ahead.

'Mind if I ask you about something very different?'
asked Carrick quietly.

'I was waiting on it.' Graham came to a halt, his
manner chilling. 'You mean my niece's death?'

Carrick nodded.

'Why?'

'Because of what's happening here,' said Carrick,
his face expressionless. 'Things are building up to a
feud, Rother's men against the rest. And I don't mean
just pin-pricks like some idiot cutting a few sharks
loose.'

Graham stood tight-lipped for a moment, then
shrugged. 'There isn't much to tell. Helen was nine-
teen, my sister's child – and with brains as well as
looks, studying geology, always collecting the odd
pebble or chipping some rock. She visited up here any
time she could and I liked it when she came. I live
alone, and she was good company.' He paused, then
added in ice-cold fashion, 'You'll have heard she was
pregnant?'

'Yes.' Carrick chose his words carefully. 'Did she
give you any hint . . . ?'

'No.' It came fiercely. 'The girl said nothing to me.
All I noticed on that last visit was that she seemed a
lot quieter than usual. Afterwards – well, the doctor
who carried out the post-mortem reckoned she'd been
nearly three months with child.'

The old-fashioned phrase carried its own built-in hurt, and by outside standards the West Coast islands clung to a fiercely Calvinistic outlook when it came to morals. For a moment Carrick wondered which mattered most to Graham – that his niece had died or that disgrace had been brought to his doorstep.

'The village think the father could be Dave Rother – or young Benson,' he said softly.

'Not because of anything I've said,' rasped Graham. 'Let's get that clear. For all I know she was sleeping with some of her university friends. I've little time for Rother or his people – they're outsiders here. But I can't judge them on that alone and if I did know the man, knew for sure, I think I'd kill him.' He held out his hands, the long, thin fingers spread wide. 'With these, Carrick – that's how I feel about it. So I've got to be sure.' His hands closed slowly again and he drew a deep breath. 'Helen wasn't a bad girl. She was more a child, a child who panicked. But the shame stays. With her and with me. And there's no more to say.'

Before Carrick could answer the tall, thin figure was stalking away from him into the dusk. An old Ford was parked a little way along the road and Graham stopped at it and climbed aboard. A moment later the engine fired, was revved hard, then slammed into gear. The car took off almost viciously, wheels scrabbling, cutting across the road in a full-lock U-turn.

Brakes squealed a protest as another approaching car swerved to avoid collision. Graham didn't slow, his engine still at full throttle, the Ford rapidly heading inland. The car he'd so nearly hit coasted to a stop beside Carrick.

'Who on earth was that maniac?' asked Sheila Francis through the opened driver's window.

'Graham from the distillery.' Carrick went over to her. 'He – well, let's say I was probing an old wound.'

'Oh.' Her voice showed an immediate understanding. Hands resting on the steering wheel, neat in her blue nursing uniform, she grimaced. 'Then let me know if you do it again. I'll make sure I'm not around.'

'Sorry.' Carrick answered absently. Till five minutes before he'd thought of Harry Graham as a fairly colourless individual with a minor mean streak. Now he felt he'd been given a brief glimpse inside the man but still wasn't completely sure of all he'd seen – except that Graham was no person to trifle with.

'What's wrong?' Sheila Francis reacted to his expression with a frown. 'Webb, if you were talking about Helen Grant . . .'

He nodded. 'You know about her?'

'Most of my patients made sure I did the first time I was seen talking to Dave.' She grimaced at the memory then looked at him again. 'Going anywhere special?'

'No.'

'Then get in.' Reaching over, she swung open the passenger door. 'I've finished my calls, but Maggie MacKenzie told me to look in on the way home. She won't mind an extra visitor – and we can talk there.'

Carrick went round, climbed in, and she set the car moving again. It was a small Health Department issue Austin and her black nursing bag was lying on the back seat.

'Whose side are you on?' she asked suddenly, her eyes on the road. 'Do you back Dave or the village?'

'I'm supposed to be a professional neutral,' he reminded her wryly.

'There's no such animal.' She changed down a gear for a bend ahead. 'I use the same line often enough but it isn't true. When it comes to Dave, I like him – but I wouldn't particularly trust him.' Her eyes flickered in his direction for a moment. 'Would you?'

Carrick shook his head but didn't answer.

The Austin travelled through the village, then slowed at the far end, turned into a narrow lane, and climbed a steep gradient for about a hundred yards. She stopped it and pulled on the handbrake outside a small, white-walled cottage with a black slate roof, a tiny garden and a view which encompassed the entire bay. Carrick got out, waited till the girl joined him, then they went together up the path to the front door. It opened as they arrived and Maggie MacKenzie stood there smiling a welcome.

'God!' The smile died as she saw him. 'Sheila, you didn't tell me you'd have a man wi' you – look at me!' She was in an old dressing gown, her feet in slippers, a scarf wrapped turban-style round her head with metal curlers showing. 'It's the night I wash my hair and – oh, come on in anyway, both of you.'

Inside the cottage was bright and neat with chintz curtains, matching chair-covers and an array of polished brass ornaments above the hearth, where a peat fire smouldered.

'Sit down now you're here.' Maggie MacKenzie waved towards the chairs, then bustled to add another cup and saucer to the tray already waiting on a table. Turning, she unplugged a bubbling coffee percolator. 'Some folk have been having a busy night, eh?'

'Meaning what, Aunt Maggie?' asked Sheila Francis. Flopping back in a chair, she removed her nursing cap and let her copper-red hair cascade around her shoulders. 'If you mean the sharks, say so, will you? I'm too tired to try guessing.'

'The sharks,' agreed the woman. She gestured towards the window, where an old brass telescope was mounted on a tripod stand with the barrel trained out towards the bay. 'I'd almost a ringside seat with that thing.'

Crossing over, Carrick used the eyepiece and adjusted the focus. A stretch of dark water leapt into close-up, then, as he eased the barrel slightly, he found himself looking at the shark-base huts on Camsha Island. They were dark shapes in the gathering night but lights were burning in most windows.

'Maggie . . .' he began.

'Coffee first,' she said firmly.

It came black from the percolator. She gave them a cup each, poured one for herself, then settled in a chair with a sigh of contentment.

'How's Mrs MacPherson's boy, Sheila?' she queried.

'Still waiting.' The girl sipped her coffee then explained for Carrick's benefit. 'He's a five-year-old who swallowed a marble.'

'Och, I wouldn't worry. It'll be like the old story about the horse and the bee.' Maggie MacKenzie ignored Carrick's unconcealed impatience and rocked gently in her chair. 'This particular bee was swallowed by the horse. So there the bee finds himself, inside the horse's stomach and as angry as Satan at a saints' reunion. But it was snug and dark and warm down there, so the bee decided to have a rest before he stung the horse. Only he went to sleep . . . and when he woke up the horse had gone!'

Carrick grinned, heard Sheila Francis chuckle, then deliberately put down his cup and pointed towards the telescope.

'All right, Maggie. What did you see?'

She considered him thoughtfully. 'I wouldn't want to get anyone into any kind of bother . . .'

'You won't. Not through me, anyway.'

'And I wouldn't like to be thought a nosy old bitch . . .'

'No.' He said it flatly. 'Let's have it, Maggie.'

'Well,' – she leaned forward almost eagerly – 'I happened to be having my usual wee look around the bay at sunset, the way I do most evenings. That was when I saw someone I thought I recognized prowling around over on Camsha Island.'

'Who?' asked Sheila Francis, puzzled.

The older woman shrugged. 'It looked like that young Peter Benson from here. He was sneaking around the huts near the slipway when I saw him – acting as if he was hiding from someone. Then I lost sight of him, an' a wee while later the shark carcasses began drifting out into the bay.'

'Benson?' Carrick stared at her. 'Are you sure?'

'I couldn't be, man. Not at that distance,' she retorted in a slightly peevish voice. 'But I still say it looked like him.'

Carrick frowned at his feet. 'He loses his job at the end of this week. So he could be trying to get his own back.'

'The lad has had a rough time all round,' mused Maggie MacKenzie. 'First he finds folk coldshouldering him over Helen Grant's death. Then those idiots from the *Harvest Lass* beat him up and while he's practically still bleeding his own boss gives him the heave.' She smiled to herself. 'Well, if he did do it good luck to him. It shows he's got some backbone.'

'Dave will kill him if he finds out,' said Sheila Francis in a worried voice.

'He may have to find him first, Sheila,' Maggie MacKenzie told her. 'You see, there's another wee thing. Just about the time the sharks started drifting I thought I saw someone leave Camsha, wading across

54

the shallows to the far side of the bay. Remember, the tide was out.'

For Carrick, it amounted to a feeling of relief. If Aunt Maggie was right then the whole incident shrank in importance. Dave Rother might howl his rage, but as long as young Benson had the sense to get well away . . .

'At least it wasn't anyone from the village,' said Sheila Francis, as if reading his mind. She eased herself with a murmur of relief and swung her long, slim legs up on the chair. 'Things are stirred up enough already.' She looked pointedly at Carrick, then turned. 'He hasn't been exactly helping, Maggie. When I found him he'd been talking to Harry Graham. You can guess why.'

'And being his usual tactful self, I imagine,' said Maggie with a heavy sarcasm. 'Men – they're a damned menace, all of them.'

Carrick shrugged defensively. 'It was worth it, Maggie. He's a lot different underneath from what I expected. I'd say he has his own kind of patience – but I wouldn't like to cross him.'

'That's sense, at least.' The woman's voice became suddenly serious. Reaching down, she silently picked up a poker from the hearth and used it to stir the smouldering peat fire. It sputtered to a fresh glow as she looked up. 'The man may not look it now, but he was a Commando in the last war. So was my own husband till he was killed – they were in the same platoon. My Andrew used to say Harry Graham never rushed anything, but that he was the one man he knew who'd rather kill with his hands than waste a bullet.'

'That's what he said he had in mind, when he's sure,' said Carrick quietly.

'Then he means it.' She laid down the poker and tucked her dressing gown closer, sitting quietly for a

55

moment as if alone with her own memories. There was a silence in the room, broken only by the soft sputter of the fire and the ticking of the clock.

'What was his niece like?' asked Sheila Francis suddenly.

'Pretty in her own way and fond of having a man around.' The tanned face wrinkled in a smile. 'Mind you, at that age I felt the same. A man's a useful thing if you keep him in his place.'

Carrick grinned wryly at the thrust. 'Was that the reason she kept coming up here?'

'Maybe part of it. Though I'd the feeling things might not be too happy at her own home. She certainly had her freedom in Portcoig. Harry Graham didn't worry about what she did and usually he was too busy at the distillery to know anyway.' She stopped, her mouth firmly resolute. 'Now that's enough about it. There's no use asking me more because I just don't know. Nobody does.'

'It might be better if it stays that way,' said Sheila Francis quietly. She uncurled from her chair. 'Is there more coffee in that pot, Aunt Maggie?'

'Help yourself.' The woman's manner became brisk again. 'I'll take some too. And now it's my turn. Webb, tell me about this Pettigrew man you've got aboard – starting with why he always looks so damnably miserable. He's not much to look at, but when you get to my age that doesn't matter so much as long as they're in trousers.'

Carrick grinned and tried to answer.

It was close to midnight when Maggie MacKenzie gave a first polite yawn. Carrick and the girl took the hint, shook their heads at her mild protests, and left the cottage minutes later.

Outside the clouds had cleared and the black velvet sky sparkled with starlight. But it was cold and the on-shore wind had built up in strength.

'I'll drive you back to the pier,' volunteered Sheila Francis as they reached her car. 'After that I'm heading straight for bed – I had to be up at dawn this morning.'

'I could always walk,' said Carrick quizzically.

'Why? I pass the pier to get home anyway,' she declared with a mild irritation. 'Look, I'm getting cold just standing here. So stop arguing and get in.'

He gave her a mock salute and obeyed. Starting the car, she turned it and drove back the way they'd come. As the long silhouette of the pier showed ahead, Carrick cleared his throat mildly.

'Any chance you'll have some time off tomorrow night?' he asked.

'I might.' She took her eyes off the road for a moment. 'Does that mean you think you'll still be here?'

'It looks that way. Maybe for longer unless things settle.'

'I see.' She frowned slightly, letting the car coast to a halt near the start of the pier. Her pert face was serious in the glow of the panel lights. 'Webb, a district nurse hears a lot. You're right. Trouble is being stirred up – stories from the way Dave owes money to different people onward. There's even been talk of the men from here going over and physically throwing the sharkmen off Camsha.'

'That sounds like Alec MacBean at his best.'

She shook her head. 'He may talk. But Fergie Lucas is the one who really has it in for Dave. Fergie is popular in the village – plenty of the younger fishermen would be right behind him if he started anything.'

'Dave Rother is fairly good at taking care of himself,' mused Carrick. 'So are his men. Lucas and his friends could find themselves up against more than they reckoned.'

'Perhaps.' Sheila Francis rubbed a slim hand along the rim of the steering wheel. Then she smiled wryly. 'I could be free about seven tomorrow, unless the telephone rings. When I get the chance I know a beach where there's not as much as an old beer can on the sand and the water's almost warm.'

'Good.' Carrick grinned, reached for the door handle, then stopped. 'Should I ask if Dave will mind?'

'No.' She shook her head and smiled. 'I'll pick you up here. Good-night, Webb.'

He climbed out and the little Austin purred off, headlamps tracing its way through the sleeping village. Lighting a cigarette, he thought over what she'd said. If Fergie Lucas tried his crazy idea of taking over the sharking base there would be a few broken heads – or worse – on either side. But for a few days at least the salvage job on the *Harvest Lass* should keep Lucas fully occupied and that might be time enough for things to cool down.

Starting along the pier, he noticed *Marlin* had a few deck lights burning and grinned. Probably one or two of the crew still had to wander back – with a clutch of hangovers to share in the morning. Though they'd try to hide the fact. While Captain Shannon turned a blind eye on a man who merely looked grey he came down like the wrath of God on anyone who couldn't disguise the rest.

Some small line-boats were clustered near the shore end of the pier. He passed them, came near to a row of three larger seine-netters tied side by side almost under *Marlin*'s bow, then came to a sudden halt.

A shadowy figure was padding around the deck of

the middle boat of the trio, working in silence near the shadowed wheelhouse in a way that held no ordinary purpose.

Dropping his cigarette and quickly grinding it out, Carrick peered into the darkness for a moment, heard a faint clink of metal on metal and then a soft gurgling. Moistening his lips, he took a few quiet steps nearer the boat.

As he did, the reek of kerosene reached his nostrils. Swearing under his breath, conscious the man below only had to glance up to see him silhouetted against the night sky, Carrick watched a moment longer. The figure on the middle boat moved again, setting down the fuel can he'd been holding, dragged something which rustled along the deck, then lifted the can and began pouring again.

Tight-lipped, Carrick reached the edge of the pier and dropped lightly to the deck of the nearest boat. He landed near the stern, hugged the shelter of her piled nets for an instant, and listened. Above the soft lapping of the water he heard a rustling, another clink of metal, then silence.

Rising, he took one look across then quit the shelter of the nets. The middle boat's deck was deserted again. But the reek of kerosene was stronger than ever.

Abandoning stealth, Carrick swung himself over the narrow gap between the two hulls, reached the seine-netter's wheelhouse, and found the fuel can lying on its side next to a kerosene-soaked pile of old fish-boxes and sacking. Beyond it, the wheelhouse door lay open, the interior an ink-black darkness broken only by the faint luminous glow from the compass binnacle.

But there was someone in there. He could sense it, could almost feel the other man's presence. Hesitating, he glanced towards *Marlin*. All the help he needed was there, but he couldn't take time to fetch it – not without giving his quarry a chance to escape.

Easing nearer the doorway he took a deep breath, tensed, then made a sudden dive forward into the wheelhouse gloom. As he did, a figure sprang from the shadows and a club sliced down at him – but the sheer speed of his entry saved Carrick. The blow intended for his head smashed against his shoulder, numbing it with pain, but still leaving him free to grapple the attacker before the club could be used again.

Struggling, the other man cursing, they went down together and grappled, rolling on the deck. Carrick collided with a metal stanchion, twisted his body away as the club slammed down again, then desperately slammed a fist into his attacker's stomach.

The blow brought a low whoop of pain. It was too dark to see the man's face, but he was medium height and strong – strong enough to come straight back in again. Carrick dodged a hand which clawed for his eyes, pistoned another blow into the man's stomach in reply, then managed to tear himself free.

Rolling clear, he started to scramble up. Then something exploded against his head and he felt himself falling while the whole world whirled. Hitting the deck planking, dazed and semi-conscious, he heard quick, heavy breathing and a scuffle of feet. A match rasped outside, there was a grunt, then the kerosene-soaked bonfire ignited in a searing blast of heat and yellow flame. Suddenly it was brighter than day around him – and the scorching tongues of fire were already leaping higher, spreading fast.

Groggily, Carrick groped around for support, felt the wood of a locker, and managed to heave himself upright. Swaying, coughing as smoke and heat seared at his lungs, he clung there for a moment in a daze while the crackling flames began to grow to a roar and the wheelhouse glass cracked and shattered with a sound like pistol-shots.

Gradually his head began to clear and he became vaguely aware of voices shouting somewhere outside. There was a fire extinguisher clipped to the bulkhead and he staggered across, pulled it loose, then turned back towards the flames.

A billow of sparks greeted Carrick as he neared the doorway. Throwing up an arm to protect his face, he lurched through into the open air and stood coughing, gasping for breath while he tried to bring the extinguisher round.

Before he could succeed, a pair of powerful arms suddenly grabbed him. Spun round bodily, he was smashed back against the deckrail.

'Here's one o' the devils,' bellowed a voice almost in his ear.

Through smoke-stung eyes he saw an angry, bearded face and a massive fist swinging back to hit him. But the blow didn't land. An even larger hand grabbed the man's arm and held it. Then Clapper Bell's face swam into his vision. The bo'sun peered incredulously, then grinned.

'It's one o' our officers, friend,' declared Bell loudly. 'Take that ruddy fire extinguisher he's got. We'll need it.'

Gladly, Carrick surrendered the fire extinguisher as the bearded fisherman released him with a muttered apology. Putting a steadying arm around him, Bell guided him back from the flames. Gradually, Carrick took in the rest. Several figures, some from *Marlin*, and the others fishermen, were already battling the blaze with extinguishers, water buckets and hastily wetted sacking. Others were on the outermost seine-netter, starting up her engine.

'We'll get you out o' this,' decided Clapper Bell. 'What the hell happened anyway, sir?'

'I tried to tackle the character who started this.' Carrick winced at the pain throbbing through his head. 'Don't ask me what he hit me with, but it felt like half of Portcoig.'

In the background the outer fishing boat's engine coughed to life and her mooring lines were slipped. She edged out, then waited, ready to tow her sister boat clear if the fire looked like spreading.

'Somebody's usin' his head,' grunted Bell. 'Come on now – it's our turn.'

Ignoring Carrick's protests, he steered him back through the milling fire-fighters, across the inner seine-netter's deck then half-pushed, half-lifted him back up to the pier. As they reached it a portable floodlamp flared to life at *Marlin*'s bow. Another moment and a hose-jet projected beside it. There was a warning shout, the fire-fighters scattered, and the hose began lancing water.

'First things first,' declared Bell, grinning again. He dragged a small flask from his hip pocket and uncapped it carefully. 'Here, sir.'

Sitting thankfully on a bollard, Carrick took a long swallow from the flask. It was neat rum, which sent him coughing. But the fierce spirit helped blast the last of the mist from his mind. He sat for a moment watching the hose-jet at work, seeing it make fast work of extinguishing the flames on the seine-netter.

'Panic over,' said Bell confidently. He retrieved the flask and took a quick swallow before he tucked it away again. 'Our bloke on gangway duty saw flames an' rang the alarm bell, so we turned out. The locals started arrivin' about the same time. Some o' them think they saw a man headin' away from the pier.' He stopped, looking past Carrick, and his expression changed. 'Here's the Old Man comin', sir. He looks fit to be tied.'

It was a reasonable description. Wearing a duffel coat over brightly patterned pyjamas, the pyjama legs tucked into sea-boots and his moon-shaped face still heavy with sleep, Captain Shannon had all the appearance of an ageing, homicidally inclined teddy bear.

Carrick tried to get to his feet as he reached them. Scowling, Shannon waved him down again.

'Stay there, mister. Stagger like that and the locals will have you drunk by morning.' He glared across at the hose-jet still playing on the seine-netter. 'All right, spell it out for me.'

Carrick did. As he finished the hose-jet was finally turned off and the waiting fishermen and *Marlin*'s fire-fighters moved in again, slapping busily with wet sacking at the last lingering tongues of flame.

Grunting, Shannon glanced along the pier, where a thickening crowd was gathering.

'Bo'sun . . .'

'Sir?' Bell stiffened, being careful not to breathe in Shannon's direction.

'Put a couple of men on keeping that mob from spilling any nearer. Then get over to that boat again and see what you can find.'

'Aye aye, sir.'

As the burly figure set off, Shannon turned to Carrick again and chewed ill-naturedly on a stray tendril of beard. 'First Rother has his sharks set adrift, then this happens over here. Tit for tat – or that's how I'd read it.' He grunted under his breath. 'Other people will too, mister. This man you saw would you know him again?'

Carrick shook his head.

Muttering under his breath, Shannon looked around then bellowed, 'Master Wills . . .'

A moment passed, then a smoke-blackened Jumbo Wills trotted to join them.

'Sir?'

'Finished playing at fire brigades?'

'Yes, sir.' Wills grinned uneasily. 'The damage isn't too bad actually and . . .'

'I'll take your word for it,' snapped Shannon, cutting him short. 'Gather up half a dozen of the hands. Make sure nothing that floats leaves this pier unless I know first.'

'Aye aye, sir.' Wills moistened his lips and hesitated. 'Suppose someone tries?'

'You stop them. Throw them off the pier. Now move!'

Wills gulped, nodded, and trotted off. Watching him go, Shannon drew a deep, groaning breath.

'Mister, I'd give a lot to know what the good Lord gave that young idiot in place of brains. If he ever gets command of anything bigger than a rowing boat . . .' He stopped, his attention suddenly switched towards the crowd being held back at the far end of the pier.

An argument of some kind seemed to have broken out. There were shouts, curses, then the men on guard were literally shoved aside and two figures marched purposefully into the smoke-laced glare of light. As Carrick recognized them he swallowed hard and struggled up to his feet.

'Here comes all we needed,' said Shannon in near disbelief. 'Rother . . .'

Another moment and Dave Rother reached them, Yogi Dunlop hovering like an escort a few paces to the rear.

'Captain, your men didn't seem too happy about letting us through,' said Rother crisply. 'But I wanted to see you – and now, not later.'

'Why?' Shannon eyed him coldly.

Rother shrugged. 'You'd soon have heard we'd been back in the village.' He thumbed towards the smoke-wreathed seine-netter. 'Some of the locals seem to have the idea that Yogi or I might have been playing with matches. I wouldn't like you to come round to the same idea.'

'It might not be hard,' answered Shannon coldly.

'Give me some credit,' sighed Rother, unperturbed. 'If ever I wanted to start a fire it would be a real one. But I've a feeling you'd go jumping to conclusions.'

'Why aren't you out at the island, Dave?' asked Carrick quietly.

'I'm on a little private errand of my own, boy.' The fair-haired sharkman's face tightened a fraction. 'A domestic thing, believe me.' Coming closer, he eyed Carrick carefully. 'You look like you caught the rough end of this deal. Doesn't he, Yogi?'

The big harpoon gunner grinned dutiful agreement.

'Still, you always had a thick skull,' mused Rother. 'I'm more worried about you, Captain. Run around in pyjamas at your age and you're inviting a chill in the bladder. You should wrap up better – we don't want to lose you.' He glanced at Carrick again. 'Just remember, I'm not involved in it. Right?'

Ignoring Shannon, he swung away back the way he'd come with Dunlop trailing at his side.

Spluttering incoherently, *Marlin*'s captain had barely recovered from the outrage by the time they'd vanished back into the crowd. Then he covered up by bellowing fresh instructions to his men aboard the seine-netters, finally calming down as Clapper Bell came clambering back up on to the pier.

A paint-blistered kerosene can in one hand, the bo'sun reached them then stopped and looked back. A small group of fishermen had climbed up after him and were waiting at the edge of the pier, muttering angrily.

'Well?' demanded Shannon. 'Any luck?'

'Some, sir.' Bell hefted the fuel can. 'He used this – it belonged to the boat, kep' in the stern locker, where you'd expect it to be.'

'And the locker forced open?'

'Aye. An' I found this, sir.' Bell held out his other hand. On his broad palm lay a heavy bone-handled clasp-knife, the hinged blade open but snapped off short, the broken piece of blade lying beside it. 'The knife was lyin' near the wheelhouse. The wee broken bit was at the stern locker.'

Shannon looked at the knife, then, lips pursed, took it from him and passed it to Carrick. In the glare cast by *Marlin*'s spotlight the initials 'D.R.' burned deep into the bone handle stood out plainly.

'Nice friends you have, mister,' grated Shannon, his round face a cold fury. 'D.R. – David Rother. For all he cared you might have been barbecued in that wheelhouse. Now you know why he came back to see if we'd found this.'

Carrick shook his head. It seemed too simple an explanation.

'Sir ...' Bell thumbed back towards the waiting fishermen. 'They know about the knife. In fact, it was one o' them found it.'

They looked over at the angry, restless group of smoke-blackened figures. One of them, stocky and scowling, gave a wolfish grin as Carrick's eyes met his own. Stepping forward, Fergie Lucas made himself spokesman.

'What about it now, eh?' he bellowed. 'You Fishery snoops get out o' the way an' we'll deal with that bastard Rother an' his stinking sharkers. We'll fix them, once an' for all.'

The men around him rumbled a noisy agreement. Shannon waited till it died, glaring at them.

'Just try it,' he invited icily. 'Try it, and I'll see every last one of you jailed – if I've got to tow you there on a raft.' Ignoring their fresh muttering he turned to Bell and lowered his voice. 'Clapper, you'll find Rother along the pier or not far away. That long-haired gunner is with him. Take a couple of men and bring them aboard *Marlin*. Knock any heads together you have to, but get them aboard in one piece. Now.'

Bell spat happily on his hands and set off.

Chapter Four

Twenty minutes passed before Rother and Yogi Dunlop were brought back. By then the crowd on the pier had thinned but there were still enough of them remaining to form a threatening, jostling escort along the pier. It took half a dozen of *Marlin*'s crew to keep the gangway clear once the two men had been taken aboard.

Captain Shannon was waiting in the spartan comfort of the Fishery cruiser's wardroom. His lack of sleep still showed, but he'd changed into uniform. Carrick joined him there, head throbbing in a lower key after a cold-water soaking, just as the shouts and jeers outside heralded the arrivals.

'Good,' said Shannon softly. Clasping his hands behind his back, he faced the wardroom door hungrily. There was a knock and it opened. Clapper Bell entered first, Dave Rother and Dunlop angrily at his heels, the seamen who'd helped bring them hovering in the companionway outside.

'Any trouble, Bo'sun?' asked Shannon curtly.

'A wee job findin' them, sir – that's all. They were up in the village,' reported Bell laconically. He glanced at Yogi Dunlop and grinned slightly. The long-haired gunner had a smear of blood on one corner of his mouth. 'Mind you, they weren't too pleased.'

'Your men dragged us here,' rasped Rother. Thin face flushed, he glared indignantly at Shannon. 'Being in command of this tub doesn't make you God, you fat old goat. Just how much do you think you can get away with?'

All expression wiped from his bearded face, Shannon ignored the shark-boat skipper. 'Stay, Bo'sun,' he ordered. 'But close that door.'

Silently, Clapper Bell obeyed then took up a strategic position beside it.

'You've some kind of complaint, Mr Rother?' asked Shannon with an icy sarcasm.

'You'll find out the hard way,' snarled Rother. 'We were grabbed in the street, roughed up, then hauled up that pier like ...' Suddenly his voice died. He stared at the broken clasp-knife Shannon had left lying on the wardroom table.

Yogi Dunlop had seen it too. He took a shuffling step nearer then stopped and glanced at Rother, his manner uneasy.

'Go on, Mr Rother,' encouraged Shannon softly.

Rother shook his head and sighed. 'Forget it. Where did you find that?'

'It was on the seine-netter,' said Carrick. Going over, he picked the knife up and held it in the flat of his hand. 'Your initials, Dave.'

'My knife,' answered Rother curtly. 'Or it was.'

'Was?' Shannon raised a cynical eyebrow. 'Meaning you lost it?'

'Gave it to someone.' Rother scowled briefly, then, without asking, dragged one of the wardroom chairs from the table and sat down. 'All right, Captain. No complaints. I'll tell you why, if you'll listen.'

'I'll listen,' agreed Shannon woodenly.

'That was my knife. Till a month ago, till I gave it to one of my crew. Correct, Yogi?'

69

Dunlop grunted agreement. 'The fool kid lost his own an' kept moaning about it. Plenty of our people knew.'

'It just happens I came ashore tonight looking for him,' said Rother grimly. 'For a separate reason, one that doesn't matter here. I haven't found him yet.'

'Peter Benson?' asked Carrick bluntly.

Rother blinked, then nodded.

'Better tell the rest, Dave,' said Carrick. He gave Shannon a mildly apologetic glance, then went on: 'You think it was Benson who cut those sharks loose and he'd vanished from Camsha when you got back, right?'

'How the hell did you know?' asked Rother almost wearily.

'Someone else had the same idea,' answered Carrick obliquely. Captain Shannon's gathering scowl held its own warning and he explained quickly, 'Benson is the youngster who was beaten up last night, sir.'

'I know that much, mister,' growled Shannon. 'What about the rest?'

'He was out of a job from the end of this week. Maybe he decided to walk out now – and wanted to leave a few reminders behind him.'

Rother nodded wryly. 'I'll admit that's how it looks to me now. The young devil was alone on the island tonight – I made him stay there. Remember I told you that, Webb?'

Considerably deflated, Shannon stood tight-lipped for a moment.

'Can you prove any of this, Rother?'

Grinning with relief, Yogi Dunlop answered for him. 'The bit about the knife is easy enough, Captain. We've over thirty men on Camsha. Most o' them could swear to it.'

70

'And he's gone,' added Rother grimly 'So has the old motor-cycle he kept in a hut on the main shore near the island.' His eyes glittered angrily. 'I'll knock hell out of the little basket if I ever get my hands on him.'

Shannon grunted and turned his attention to Carrick. 'Couldn't you have told me some of this before, mister?' he asked curtly.

'I didn't have the chance,' reminded Carrick defensively. 'Anyway, I didn't know how it fitted, sir.'

Beginning to enjoy the situation, Rother chuckled. 'I warned you about going off half-cocked, Shannon,' he reminded, loafing back in the chair. 'You should have listened. Now how about telling that mob waiting on the pier they're wasting their time?'

A knock on the wardroom door robbed Shannon of a chance to reply. It opened and Pettigrew entered with an unhappy expression.

'Well?' demanded Shannon.

'We've got a fishermen's deputation at the gangway, sir,' reported the middle-aged junior second unenthusiastically. 'They want to see you.' His eyes flickered towards the two sharkmen. 'They're demanding to know what's happening.'

'Demanding?' Shannon bristled at the word. 'Damn their impudence. Tell them to go to . . .' He stopped and sighed. 'No, better not. Not right now. All right, I'll see them. While I'm doing that, I've a job for you.'

'Me, sir?' Pettigrew didn't quite groan.

'You.' Shannon turned to Dave Rother. 'Did you bring a boat over?'

Rother nodded. 'We've a dinghy along the pier.'

'Right.' Shannon swung back to Pettigrew. 'They'll give you a full description of a man called Peter Benson. Then make sure they get to that dinghy in one piece.'

71

Pettigrew nodded, then remembered his other reason for coming. 'We've still a shore-leave man adrift, sir. It's Halliday.'

'Again?' murmured Carrick and grinned. One of the engine-room greasers, Gibby Halliday always turned up eventually. But even when sober his blood-alcohol content would probably be impressive.

'Damn Halliday,' snapped Shannon. 'Put him on report, man. Carrick, you'd better come with me till I fix this deputation. We'll bring them aboard – that'll give Pettigrew more of a chance to get these two ashore.'

He stumped out of the wardroom. Following, Carrick grimaced a wry farewell towards Dave Rother. The sharkman raised one hand in a laconic acknowledgement then gave a heavy wink.

Rother, at least, seemed unworried. But following Shannon along the companionway Carrick had doubts of his own.

The figure he'd grappled with in the darkness of that wheelhouse might conceivably have been young Benson. But his opponent had been viciously determined, and cool enough to start the fire before making his escape.

Somehow none of that fitted with his own notion of Peter Benson's character. Even if all the rest fitted. And he was still puzzled about the way he'd been struck, by a blow that might have come out of nowhere.

'We haven't got all night, mister,' said Shannon suddenly, cutting across his thoughts. *Marlin*'s captain had reached the companionway door that led to the main deck and was waiting on him. 'Let's get this over with. Then I'll get that young idiot's description off to the civil police. At least we're on an island – he won't find it easy to get off.'

* * *

72

The fishermen's deputation, when they came aboard, were four in number. All were skippers, two from local boats and two from Mallaig boats using the bay, all were older men of the type any Fishery Protection captain took seriously.

Shannon led them to his day-cabin, opened a bottle, and poured them each a drink. They thanked him, sipped slowly in dignified style, then the oldest, elected spokesman, came straight to the point.

'Are you locking up those sharkers, Captain?'

'No. But we're looking for one of their men who had a grudge against a few people – young Benson,' said Shannon bluntly. 'He seems to have bolted.'

'That one, eh?' The skipper's leathery face showed an understanding and he glanced at his companions. 'The lad who fathered that bairn – aye, it makes sense.' On the strength of the information he emptied his glass at a single gulp. 'Even so, I've a duty to give you a warning, Captain. The fishing fleet aroun' this part o' the inch has had its fill o' these sharkmen, one way an' another.'

'I see.' Shannon reached for the bottle again, but stopped as the man shook his head. 'I'd have thought men like you would have more sense than ...'

'Not us, Captain.' The skipper held up a hand to stop him. 'But we've younger men wi' less patience.'

'And Fergie Lucas leading them?' suggested Carrick.

The man nodded. 'Him among others, Chief Officer. One more wee incident like tonight an' Satan himself won't stop them taking those sharkmen apart.'

'And we won't particularly feel like stoppin' them,' grunted another of the skippers.

Shannon kept his temper, but his voice took on a new edge. 'You'd better think about that one again. Or

73

the only fishing you'd do afterwards would be with a piece of string and a bent pin off the edge of the pier. That's a promise.'

'You might be there too, Captain,' murmured the spokesman. 'That Department o' yours likes things nice an' peaceful. The way they saw it, they might give someone else the job o' driving that fine big boat o' yours.'

'I've heard that before – and I'll hear it again.' Shannon looked at the man for a moment, then, surprisingly, gave a sound close to a chuckle. 'So to hell with you too, Skipper. Now we know where we stand, do we have that other drink?'

The fishermen glanced at each other their manner uncertain. Then, grinning shamefacedly, they nodded in turn.

Before they left the bottle had gone round a third time. But it had been worth it. Their attitudes slightly thawed, the four skippers went away promising they'd at least try to calm things down among the crews.

Shannon saw them ashore. When he came back he grimaced at Carrick and yawned.

'That's it for tonight, mister. Better get some sleep.'

'I will,' agreed Carrick. 'Any sign of Gibby Halliday, sir?'

'Not yet.' Shannon sniffed heavily at the reminder. 'He'll keep till morning, then I'm going to have his guts, drunk or sober.'

Gibby Halliday turned up soon after dawn. The last boats of the fishing fleet were leaving, heading out of the bay for the start of another day's work, when the wash from a propeller blade brought his body drifting sluggishly from the dark shelter of the pier.

They brought him up to the pier and laid him there, a scrawny figure in off-duty sweat-shirt and slacks. A bottle still protruded from his hip pocket and the bold, tattooed figure of an anatomically provocative female mocked them from one hairy arm while water from his clothes formed a growing pool on the planks below.

It was easy enough to see how he'd died. His head had been smashed in, the skull almost pulped under what must have been a rain of blows.

Jumbo Wills was *Marlin*'s officer of the watch. He was on the pier when the dead greaser was taken out of the water and came back aboard looking sick. Already up and dressed, Carrick got to the spot minutes later, pushed his way through the men clustered round the body, and found Captain Shannon standing there, staring down.

'Drunk or sober,' said Shannon, almost to himself. His mouth tightened bitterly. 'He must have been coming back when your damned firebug was escaping. Probably never even knew what was happening – just got in the way.'

'Does Andy Shaw know?' asked Carrick quietly. Gibby Halliday had been one of the chief engineer's squad for a long time.

'I've sent for him.' Shannon drew a long breath. 'Rother's boats have left base. But get out there and talk to anyone you find. I want any lead we can on this Peter Benson. God help him if some of the crew get their hands on him before the shore police do.'

Andy Shaw was arriving as Carrick left. Unshaven, rumpled enough to have slept in his clothes, *Marlin*'s chief engineer headed past without a word. Face the colour of paper, he walked like a man who didn't want to get where he was going.

Even when sober, Gibby Halliday would have shared his last cigarette with any man. Shannon was right. Guilty or not, Peter Benson would have short shrift and find little mercy if he fell into the hands of the dead greaser's friends. No amount of discipline could change that.

Passing the empty, fire-damaged seine-netter, now lying alone with her superstructure charred and blackened, Carrick went aboard the Fishery cruiser.

Five minutes later, aided by a group of grim-faced deckhands who didn't need any urging, he had the ship's motor-whaler in the water and her falls slipped. With three seamen aboard as crew he gunned the whaler's engine and sent it arcing away from *Marlin*'s side until the bow pointed straight for Camsha Island.

Clear of the pier, the lumpy swell began to toss them about. The sky overhead was grey and the wind had risen several points overnight. Instinctively he glanced towards the mouth of the bay and saw white breakers forming a foaming line along the shoal rocks.

It would be a lot rougher out in the open sea. He thought briefly of the additional difficulties for the *Heather Bee* and her crew on their salvage bid, then dismissed the thought as the seaman nearest him leaned forward.

'Do we turn the place over when we get there, sir?' asked the man hopefully. 'I was thinking, maybe those sharkers have this kid hidden away somewhere.'

Carrick shook his head. 'I want one of you to stay with the boat. The other two can look around. But no heavy stuff. Understood?'

The seaman's face fell but he nodded, then cursed as a wavecrest took them on the starboard bow, drenching a curtain of spray over the whaler. Carrick watched him for a moment. There might be more than one kind of problem ahead . . . with *Marlin*'s crew a prominent factor.

All because of one dead teenage girl.

The slipway at Camsha Island was deserted as the motor-whaler nosed in past the clutter of long black basking-shark carcasses, each moored to an oil-drum buoy. Another shark, about thirty feet long and a male, had been winched out of the water and lay on a trolley halfway up the slipway ready to be moved on to the processing plant.

The smell was the worst part of it. Heavy and rancid, it met their nostrils as soon as they'd tied up and were ashore. But it was a smell that meant money once the shark livers had been boiled down and their oil extracted and barrelled.

The rest of the carcass was usually towed out to sea and dumped. City experts talked wisely about other by-products, commercial ways of using everything from the coarse, sandpaper-like skin to the rows of tiny, needle-pointed teeth, of the protein in the flesh and the fertilizer possibilities of anything left over.

Maybe that would come. But right now all there was came down to the smell . . . and a multitude of black flies which buzzed around as Carrick and the two seamen walked towards the nearest of the huts.

'Lookin' for someone?' called a voice.

They stopped and a small man in overalls limped across from a dump of fuel drums. A cigarette dangled from his lips and his overalls were smeared yellow and red with crusted fluid and blood. He saw one of the seamen sniff as he came near and grinned.

'Name's Len Hastings. You try wadin' up to your armpits in shark liver an' you'll stink as much as I do.' He glanced keenly at Carrick. 'Got some word o' that kid Benson? Dave Rother's out wi' the boats, but I could radio him.'

'Nothing yet.' Carrick looked around. 'Left on your own?'

'No, tea-break time.' The man brushed a fly from his face with a practised flick. 'We've a brew-up near the fuel dump. Diesel oil smells a treat after this lot. Anything I can do, Chief?'

Carrick nodded. 'Where did Benson sleep?'

'End hut, end cubicle. Help yourself.'

Gesturing the seamen to stay, Carrick set off along a sandy path which led through coarse, tufted grass. He reached the hut, found the door lying open, and went into a long, narrow corridor with cubicles lying off it all along one side. The place smelled of disinfectant and the floor was scrubbed clean, signs that Dave Rother hadn't forgotten all of his Navy background.

Like the rest, Benson's cubicle had a curtain over the doorway. He shoved it back, went in, and raised a mild eyebrow at the array of magazine pin-ups pasted round the walls. Benson seemed to have a predilection for blondes and bosoms. Grinning at one which had acquired a pencilled moustache, he glanced around.

The bunk bed still had its blankets folded, but was creased as if someone had been lying on top of it. When he opened the tall locker beside the bed he found a dark suit and other clothes hanging on the rail and some laundered shirts lying on a shelf. Turning away, he kicked a pair of light tan shoes which had been placed neatly beneath the cubicle's window.

Puzzled, frowning, he prowled the rest of the space. Everything was in place, as if Peter Benson had just walked out and might return in a moment.

A small suitcase under the bunk told the same story,

down to a savings bank book with a credit of a few pounds. The bank book gave Benson a Glasgow address. Thoughtfully, Carrick put it in his pocket, then added a snapshot photograph which showed the tall, thin youngster grinning at the camera with a catcher-boat in the background.

Nothing else looked likely to help. Closing the case, he pushed it under the bed again and left the hut.

Outside, a winch engine had begun clattering. Going back along the path, Carrick reached the slip-way in time to see the trolley-mounted basking shark being dragged by a wire cable into the entrance to the main processing shed, a few men in stained overalls guiding it along. *Marlin*'s two seamen were watching, Len Hastings by their side, more flies than ever annoying them.

'Find what you wanted, Chief?' asked Hastings as Carrick reached them.

'Enough to get by on,' said Carrick non-committally.

'Good.' Face screwed into an expression of sympathy, the little man raised his voice above the noise of the engine and the squeal of the trolley wheels. 'Your lads told us about that engine-room bloke bein' killed. That's bad – but it just doesn't figure. Not wi' young Benson.'

'Why?' The trolley and its carcass were inside the shed. Carrick waited while the doors slammed shut. 'He had a king-sized chip on his shoulder, hadn't he?'

Hastings nodded wryly. 'True enough, Chief. An' the boss givin' him the chop didn't help. But I still can't see him belting anyone's skull in. An' at least the boss had promised him his back pay – that's better than the rest o' us were getting, believe me.'

Behind them, the ratings shuffled impatiently and swatted at the buzzing flies. Carrick tried lighting a cigarette, but it didn't help much.

'Money's short?'

'Has been for months.' The little man grimaced. 'Still, the boss says things will be okay pretty quick now, so we're hangin' on.' He chuckled gloomily. 'All hang together or all hang separate, that's how it is. At least we've managed to squeeze beer money out o' him.'

'Necessities first,' agreed Carrick. He thanked Hastings, signalled the two ratings, and they retreated thankfully down the slipway, away from the smell and the flies.

The shark-catching game wasn't all open-sea adventure or salt-spray excitement.

Maggie MacKenzie's little ferry launch was buzzing across the water on some errand as the motor-whaler came in towards Portcoig. She raised an arm and shouted something, but it was lost on the wind and the launch was bucking in the waves.

The swell was considerably less near the pier and the motor-whaler came neatly alongside *Marlin*. At the Fishery cruiser's stern, Clapper Bell was just in the act of climbing down a ladder. He was wearing full scuba gear and a rubber wet-suit and he paused, face-mask shoved back and breathing tube dangling loose, till the motor-whaler was near him.

'The Old Man's got me checkin' under the pier round about where Gibby Halliday got tossed in,' he reported. 'You should see the junk lyin' down there. And there's a ruddy great conger eel sniffin' around with razor-blades for teeth.'

'Kick it on the snout,' advised Carrick cheerfully. 'Any luck, Clapper?'

The bo'sun snorted. 'Enough chunks of scrap iron to start a business. Hell, I don't even know what I'm lookin' for. The Old Man's on the bridge. You can tell him I'm havin' one more go, but if that eel gets nasty he can expect me straight back.'

Face-mask down, he bit on the breathing tube and went backwards into the water with a splash. Then he vanished, his progress marked by a bubble-trail leading along the edge of the pier.

Leaving the ratings to hoist the whaler aboard, Carrick scrambled up on deck and headed for the bridge. On the way there were plenty of signs, from the mooring lines being thinned onward, which pointed to the Fishery cruiser being ready to sail. It was the same when he reached the bridge. Pettigrew was there with the duty helmsman and a brace of look-outs; Captain Shannon's cap was lying on the command chair.

'He's back there,' said Pettigrew morosely, thumbing towards the little chartroom aft. 'Don't stand on his toes. Things are bad enough.'

Carrick went through and found Shannon already had company in the bulky, uniformed shape of Sergeant Fraser. The policeman contented himself with a nod and waited.

'Learn anything, mister?' asked Shannon bluntly.

'We've these, sir.' Carrick laid the bank book and snapshot on the chartroom table. 'He'd left most of his kit behind.'

Shannon grunted. 'Anything else?'

'Just that he can't have much money. The sharkers haven't been paid for a spell.' Carrick glanced at Sergeant Fraser. 'Any trace of Benson yet?'

'Damn all sign of him or that motorbike.' The policeman shook his head gloomily. 'We're watching the ferry crossings and the usual. But out here we've only got one cop to God knows how many miles of heather. Now,' – his gloom deepened – 'well, I was on my way here when I heard about your crewman.

81

I can't cope with murder on top o' the rest. Head-quarters are sending a CID squad from the mainland.'

'Which could take long enough.' Shannon was unimpressed. He stopped as Pettigrew stuck his head round the door and snatched the radio-room flimsy the junior second offered. A glance at it and he handed the flimsy back. Then, as Pettigrew left, he went straight on: 'You'd better take that bank book and photograph, Sergeant. And anything you want from the old iron the bo'sun has been bringing up.'

Sergeant Fraser nodded. 'The old faithful blunt instrument. The forensic people can play wi' them, Captain. And I'll make the arrangements for the autopsy on Halliday.' He shrugged slightly. 'Twice in twenty-four hours – that's pretty good going.'

'John MacBean's death is now officially accidental,' said Shannon sardonically. 'The post-mortem confirmed it – and that he'd a gutful of beer. That's what brought the sergeant over, to tell us.'

'We'll still need a fatal-accident inquiry before a sheriff,' reminded Fraser quickly. 'But that's a formality now.'

'Like it was with Helen Grant?' asked Carrick, unable to stop himself.

Fraser glared at him then turned deliberately to Shannon. 'You're sailing, Captain, so I won't hold you back,' he said grimly. 'MacBean's body is being released today, they're planning the funeral here tomorrow afternoon – and I'd like it if you'd tell Rother's sharkers to stay away. For their own sake.'

Nodding curtly, he strode off. An odd rumbling noise came from Shannon's throat and he combed a hand over his beard.

'Mister . . .' He changed his mind. 'Oh, never mind. Get Clapper Bell back aboard, all hands stand ready to clear harbour. We're going out.'

'Sir?'

'We may have a man dead, but Department still say we should be working,' grated Shannon. 'That damned oil-slick has turned up again.' He flicked a finger at the chart in front of him. 'Here, on the fifty-fathom line north of Oigh Sgeir lighthouse, and the keepers are tracking it.'

Carrick raised an eyebrow. The slick had moved a long way since the last report. But he could think of better things to do than go chasing it.

'Taken root, mister?' asked Shannon heavily. 'Or do you want it in writing?'

'No, sir.' He spoke to empty air. Shannon had already left. Carrick shrugged and reached for the intercom phone.

Marlin slipped away from the pier at 0950 hours, swung on a west-south-west course once she'd cleared Camsha Bay, and built up quickly to full speed. With her shallow draught that meant tossing and rolling as she bored through the lumping seas which drenched along her decks. At her stern, the Fishery ensign snapped and flapped in the wind while her radio aerial lines sang a thin protest over the roar of the diesels.

As always, the vibrating power had a quickly soothing effect on Shannon. He was sipping coffee in the command chair and telling the beginnings of a story from the 'Bishop and the Duchess' seam when the slim white finger of Oigh Sgeir light appeared ahead. At the same time as the radio room patched through the crackling voice of the head lighthouse keeper the starboard look-out spotted the slick.

'Tell him we've got it,' ordered Shannon, setting aside his cup. 'All right, mister. Let's see if those damned hose-booms fall off this time.'

Grinning, Carrick passed the word on the bridge intercom. By the time they'd swung round to circle the slick the hose-booms were out, like two giant broomsticks, and Jumbo Wills was standing by over his charges.

It was a small slick, roughly a quarter-mile long, but narrow, a dirty blue-black ribbon on the grey sea with fragmented flotsam and a few dead seabirds trapped in its sticky grip. Occasionally a wave which wouldn't be smothered by its presence broke through, throwing congealed lumps of semi-solid into the air.

Breaking it up took about an hour and a half. First they came in close and used a sampling can on a line. That was for later, when Department chemists would analyse the sample and try to trace its origin. If the ship concerned could be traced the owners were liable to find themselves on the heavy end of considerable penalties.

Then it was the turn of the hose-booms. Keeping the slick to leeward, *Marlin* swept systematically up and down its length with the detergent sprays operating. Gradually the slick lost its form and shape and began to lump, disintegrate, and gradually sink.

At last Shannon was satisfied. The hose-booms secured, *Marlin*'s siren blew a farewell blast as they swung away from the lighthouse, and Carrick had a dog-leg course ready which would take them back to Portcoig.

Pettigrew changed that within minutes when he brought along another message from the radio room. One glance at it and Shannon stiffened in his command chair.

'Starboard helm, bring her round to 035 degrees,' he ordered sharply. 'Full power.'

As the helmsman brought the Fishery cruiser curving on her new course and the engine-room telegraph clanged, Shannon crumpled the radio message into a tight ball and turned to Carrick.

'Rother again, mister. There's a Mallaig skipper on the air howling that the *Seapearl* is trying to sink him. Then some jabber about nets and sharks.' He threw the crumpled paper across the bridge and scowled. 'God knows what's going on, but we'll get there and knock their heads together.'

The sky had cleared and the sun was breaking through, highlighting the scene, when they saw the two boats almost dead ahead. Using the bridge glasses, Carrick whistled softly between his teeth.

Seapearl and a big, yellow-hulled drifter were stationary in the water, rolling in the swell with less than a stone's-throw distance between them. Figures were running about on both boats – and the shark-catcher's harpoon gun was pointed squarely at the drifter's wheelhouse!

Behind him, Shannon had seen it too. The little hunched figure in the command chair swore crudely.

'Let them know we're here, mister,' he ordered. 'Then muster a boarding party. We're going to need it.'

White wake foaming astern, *Marlin* raced on while her siren boomed a warning. The reaction on the two boats was identical: a momentary pause while the figures on deck turned to stare, then renewed activity. As the distance closed Carrick could see a steady rain of missiles going in both directions, from chunks of wood to tin cans. The harpoon gun on the shark-catcher stayed trained as before, with Yogi Dunlop's bulky shape crouching for shelter behind its mounting.

'Boats approaching to port, sir,' reported one of the lookouts.

85

Shannon checked and grunted. Rother's two sister shark-catchers were plugging in the direction of the mêlée, still about a mile distant but coming on as fast as they could. He looked at the scene ahead then suddenly chuckled into his beard.

'Get those hose-booms out again, mister,' he ordered. 'Keep them at a forty-five-degree lift. Helmsman, fancy playing thread the needle?'

The helmsman blinked then grinned his understanding and nursed the wheel round a fraction.

'Maintain speed, sir?' queried Carrick in a deadpan voice, reaching for the intercom phone.

'Maintain speed,' confirmed Shannon. 'Stand by detergent sprays. Tell them to jump to it, mister.'

The hose-booms were angled out and ready when the distance was down to less than a cable's length. *Marlin*'s siren boomed again, but the battle ahead showed no sign of slacking.

'In we go then,' said Shannon softly, sliding down from his chair and balancing beside the helmsman. 'Watch our paintwork, laddie. Mr Carrick, sprays ready?'

'Standing by,' confirmed Carrick, the intercom at his lips.

With little more than two hundred yards to go the fishermen ahead suddenly seemed to realize what was happening. The hail of missiles between the two boats died and faces stared open-mouthed at the Fishery cruiser's apparent head-on rush.

'Ease to starboard . . . back . . . that's it,' encouraged Shannon, eyes glued ahead. 'Now damp them down, mister!'

'Sprays on,' ordered Carrick.

Detergent jetting from her angled booms, *Marlin* cut through between the two fishing boats with the gap on either side so narrow it seemed a man could have jumped across. As the detergent swept its path the fishermen scattered for cover, throwing up their hands to protect themselves, slipping and falling, shouting curses while *Marlin* rocketed through. Then her churning wake hit the smaller craft like a hammer-blow, throwing them around like corks in a bathtub and leaving their shattered crews clinging to any support they could find.

'Reduce speed to half ahead,' ordered Shannon happily. He slapped the helmsman on the back as the telegraph rang. 'Nicely done, laddie. Bring her round.'

Engine revolutions falling, *Marlin* began a wide circle in answer to her helm. Both boats were wallowing in the continuing swell, all signs of fight gone from the figures still staggering on their detergent-soaked decks.

'Secure hose-booms, sir?' asked Carrick, feeling fairly shattered himself. One slip of judgement on Shannon's part and the result could have been disaster.

'Secure booms,' confirmed Shannon, grinning. 'Mister, I want both skippers brought aboard as soon as we're alongside.' The grin faded. 'Then we'll sort this little lot out, believe me.'

Chapter Five

Five minutes and a few loud-hailer exchanges later the two feuding boats were tied up one on either side of *Marlin*, fenders rubbing against the Fishery cruiser's sides as they rolled with the swell. Beefy and red-faced, the skipper of the Mallaig drifter was first to climb aboard. He reached the fo'c'sle deck and stood belligerently, still drenched from head to foot in detergent spray. Then, as Dave Rother clambered over the starboard side and crossed the deck, the Mallaig man gave a deep-throated growl and seemed ready to start things all over again.

'Cool it,' said Carrick wearily, planting himself firmly between the two antagonists. 'You're in enough trouble and the Old Man's on his way.'

Rother shrugged, unimpressed. But the drifter skipper subsided a little, muttering to himself. Glancing past them, Carrick wryly noted the support both men had waiting on the sidelines. Rother's two sister shark-boats were hovering about two cable lengths astern. Over on the port side other company was arriving in the shape of a cluster of assorted seine-netters and line-boats, keeping their distance but hungry to know what was going on.

'Base radioed me one of your men is dead,' said Rother suddenly. He grimaced. 'Hell, you don't really think it could have been young Benson, do you?'

'We'll maybe know when we find him,' said Carrick grimly, then eased back a fraction as Captain Shannon stumped along the deck towards them.

'You,' said Shannon curtly, pointing to the Mallaig man and ignoring Rother. 'Who are you and what started this piece of idiocy?'

'Name of Craig, skipper of the drifter *Moonchild*,' snarled the Mallaig man. 'Captain, let's see Fishery Protection earn its keep. This bloody maniac tried to ram us.'

'Ask him why,' suggested Rother coldly.

Shannon glanced at him briefly, then swung back to Skipper Craig. 'Well?'

Craig licked his lips a fraction and looked uncomfortable. 'Ach, one of his damned shark-markers got tangled in our nets. We were cutting it loose that's all.'

'Was it?' demanded Shannon.

'There happened to be thirty feet of dead shark on the end of the thing,' answered Rother dryly, tucking his thumbs in the waistband of his slacks.

'It has still fouled our nets, damn you,' rasped the Mallaig man, his face getting redder. 'Should I lose a whole set o' gear over one o' your sharks?'

'Anything more to it, Dave?' asked Carrick neutrally.

'A lot.' Rother nodded and stood silent for a moment while the rope fenders creaked on either side. 'Look, you know how we work. We nail a shark, hitch a flag-buoy marker on our end of the harpoon line, leave it, and start hunting again. Either we collect on the way back and tow in a string of the brutes or we radio another of the boats to do the job.' He gave a bitter glance at the drifter skipper. 'Except lately all we've come back to is a drifting buoy and a cut line . . . and this time we caught someone at it.'

89

'An' I've told you why,' bellowed Skipper Craig indignantly. 'Don't blame me for the rest, Rother. If folk aroun' the islands wish your guts would rot out that's not my doing.' Turning, he spread his hands appealingly to Shannon. 'Captain, the man's a bloody lunatic. Before he tried to ram us he fired on us wi' that damned gun. Suppose he'd hit us?'

'All right,' rasped Shannon impatiently. 'Rother, your turn. Did that happen?'

'Two practice harpoon sticks and Yogi aimed wide.' Rother grinned slightly. 'If he'd wanted, he could have planted the real thing right up this idiot's fat . . .'

'That's enough.' Shannon glanced away and cleared his throat quickly.

'What happened to your nets, Skipper?' asked Carrick, stifling a grin.

'We cut them an' ran.' Skipper Craig shuffled his feet and looked sheepish. 'They're back there somewhere.'

'Britain's maritime glory,' murmured Rother with a heavy sarcasm.

Shannon grunted and stuck his hands in his jacket pockets. 'Rother, I'm putting your boat under arrest. You'll return to Portcoig.' He saw the Mallaig skipper begin to grin and sniffed. 'No need for you to look so happy. The same applies to you. Mr Carrick . . .'

'Sir?'

'Take a couple of men and take charge on Rother's boat. I'll put Pettigrew on the drifter.'

'What about my gear?' protested the drifterman.

'You can pick it up on the way.' Shannon considered the collection of boats around them. 'That's it for now, Mr Carrick. I'll break up the spectators. You'll find us back at Portcoig.'

* * *

Their unwelcome Fishery Protection passengers aboard, the lines holding the fishing boats were slipped. As they drew clear *Marlin*'s diesels quickened and she started off, curving towards the nearest of the hovering flotilla.

'That's it, Dave,' said Carrick wryly, grabbing a stanchion aboard the *Seapearl* as the Fishery cruiser's wash sent them lurching deeper in the swell. 'You heard the man. We go back.'

Balancing beside him, Rother gave a short chuckle which held an amused malice. 'Then get on with it,' he invited caustically. 'Earn your keep – Shannon hasn't done me any favours.'

Shrugging, Carrick took stock. The half-dozen men of the shark-catcher's crew were clustered in a scowling group near the wheelhouse. He'd brought Clapper Bell and a rating named Logan, a quietly dependable hand who'd once been a fisherman.

'Take the helm,' he told Logan. As the man edged past into the wheelhouse Carrick turned to the muttering group. 'Break it up. Some of you get a hose working. I want that detergent shifted before it settles.'

They didn't react for a moment. Then one cleared his throat and spat carefully over the side.

'You heard,' rumbled Clapper Bell. 'Move.'

Silent, they stayed where they were and Dave Rother chuckled, saying nothing.

'Then maybe one o' you feels like doin' something different,' declared Bell with a heavy scowl. 'Who's the brave lad? Let's have him, if you've anyone with guts enough.'

Suddenly, Yogi Dunlop shoved forward from the rest. The harpoon gunner's clothes were still sodden with detergent and his long hair was matted.

'You?' asked Bell hopefully.

91

'Me, you big-mouthed ape,' snarled the gunner.

Carrick felt an elbow nudge his side.

'I'll bet five quid on Yogi,' murmured Rother.

Smiling slightly, watching the two big men beginning to circle one another in almost ritualistic style, Carrick hesitated, then nodded. 'You're covered,' he agreed out of the corner of his mouth. 'Get your money out.'

Suddenly the circling ended as Yogi Dunlop lunged forward with his fists swinging. A wild left hook took Clapper Bell to the side of the jaw and the bo'sun staggered, lost his balance on the detergent-greased deck, then slithered backward to thud against the wheelhouse.

Shaking his head slightly, he recovered quickly, then came forward with the next roll of the deck. The extra momentum took him smashing into the harpoon gunner and this time it was Dunlop who went sprawling, ending up in the scuppers as a wave broke against the shark-catcher's side, drenching both men and their audience in spray.

Dunlop hauled himself to his feet, dived for Clapper Bell like an angry bull, and got in one thudding blow at the bo'sun's middle. Bell hardly blinked, side-stepped clear of the next, and they began circling again to a chorus of encouragement from the sharkman's crew-mates.

Then it was Clapper Bell's turn. Dodging a crotch-aimed kick from his opponent, he pounced quickly, grabbed a full handful of that long, matted hair, yanked in a way that almost tore it out by the roots, then smashed his free fist like a piston under the man's exposed jaw.

Eyes suddenly glazing, Dunlop wobbled with his mouth hanging open. Still gripping the man's hair, Clapper Bell swung him bodily round, rammed him

92

hard against the wheelhouse then pistoned a single forearm smash into Dunlop's belt-line.

He let go . . . and Dunlop slid slowly down the wheelhouse wood until he met the deck.

'Now,' declared Clapper Bell cheerfully, glancing round. 'Like Mr Carrick said, we want a hose. Right?'

The *Seapearl*'s crew showed no further interest in arguing.

'About that five quid,' said Dave Rother a little later. He was sprawled back on the bunk in his tiny cabin below and fractionally aft of the wheelhouse, smoking a cigarette. A mug of coffee in one hand, Carrick was leaning against a bulkhead and looking through the only porthole. The *Seapearl* was tossing and rolling along, heading at a plugging eight knots for Portcoig. 'Mind waiting a few days, Webb?'

'No, it's all right.' Outside the porthole the sea was becoming lumpier by the moment. But in contrast the sky had cleared to a brilliant, almost dazzling blue with only a few tendrils of white cloud being streaked along by the gusting westerly wind. 'Money tight?'

'If you've asked around you'll know it is.' Rother waved his cigarette expressively. 'Nothing to worry about. I've a deal coming up that will take care of things, and a fat cheque due for last month's shipment of shark-oil. But right now I'm next best thing to flat broke.'

'What kind of deal is it?'

Rother grinned and shook his head. 'You'll hear when it happens. Let's leave it that way.' His face clouded slightly. 'But one thing is certain, I'll be quitting this part of the world . . . and to hell with it in the passing.'

Carrick raised an eyebrow. 'Going away altogether?'

'Uh-huh. What's happened with young Benson puts the lid on things.' Rother eased up on his elbows, looked ready to add something more, then tensed at a shout from the wheelhouse.

It came again, an excited bellow. 'Sharko, boss – a big 'un! Port side – do we go for him?'

Scrambling from the bunk, Rother dived for the porthole. He stared, swore, and pointed for Carrick's benefit. A great black triangular sail was moving slowly through the wavecrests about four hundred yards away. It vanished briefly then reappeared, still travelling almost parallel with the *Seapearl*.

'Look at that dorsal-fin!' Eyes glinting eagerly, Rother swung round. 'Webb, how about one try? Just one – and to hell with Shannon.'

Carrick hesitated. The great black fin out there had to be at least five feet from its limp tip to the thickening base. The creature beneath had to be a giant of its kind, a giant that could vanish again at any moment.

'One try,' urged Rother. 'That's all.'

The temptation was too much. Carrick nodded. 'One try. Better make it good.'

'We will.' Rother was already at the door. Another moment and he was running along the deck, shouting orders as he went.

The shabby, paint-blistered shark-boat swung into action with a practised precision, each man of her crew knowing his task. Shoving his way behind the helm, Dave Rother swung the *Seapearl*'s blunt bow and almost simultaneously began juggling with the engine throttle. Slowing, shuddering as she took a couple of heavy seas broadside on, the boat first dropped back a little, then increased speed on a new, curving course, which meant she was now pursuing that still lazy black fin from astern.

Crammed beside Rother in the wheelhouse, Carrick saw two figures struggling with the harpoon gun on its crude bow platform. A wave drenched over them, then the spray cleared and he blinked. Yogi Dunlop had a new, unexpected assistant gunner. Beside him on the platform, shielding a box of powder cartridges from the spray, Clapper Bell was enjoying himself.

'Yogi . . .' Rother yelled through the wheelhouse doorway and waited till the man half-turned. 'Double load. And take the brute close. Right?'

Dunlop grinned and waved. The long harpoon stick, tipped with a foot of barbed, fine-honed steel, was already waiting in the muzzle. Doubling-up on the powder charge would do awesome things to its effectiveness if a man didn't object to the possibility of blowing the whole gun off its mounting.

'He's gaining on us,' murmured Carrick.

Rother peered ahead at the black dorsal-fin and frowned as he eased the throttle levers forward a fraction.

'Too fast and we'll scare him, Webb. That should do it.'

The engine beat increased. Then, above it, came an odd, rough note which made Carrick wince.

'Prop-shaft, Dave . . .'

'Prop,' corrected Rother ruefully. 'I know. We've had it before. But we'll last out. At least . . .' He stopped and cursed.

The big dorsal-fin was slowly submerging again. It slipped beneath the waves, was gone for a full minute while the *Seapearl* thudded on, then reappeared as lazily but now slightly to starboard. Relaxing, Rother corrected the shark-boat's helm and the gap gradually closed.

'Look at him now,' he said tensely. 'He's big all right.'

Gliding along just below the surface, the basking-shark's elephantine bulk seemed to stretch for ever. Swimming placidly, a great black living mass, it had to be at least fifty feet long, almost barrel-shaped, the head fringed by distended gills and tipped by snout-like jaws. It was the *cearbhan* of Gaelic fishing legends, the cursed, net-wrecking muldoan, sailfish, sunfish – there were plenty of other names – prehistoric in its size, ponderous, almost ridiculously fearsome by its very existence.

'Keep like that, damn you,' murmured Rother, nursing the throttles again. *Seapearl*'s bow drew level with a vast spread of tail, crept further along, closer and still closer through the heaving seas until the boat was almost scraping the creature's side. At the bow, Yogi Dunlop had the harpoon gun swung round and crouched tensely, waiting.

Suddenly the great sail-fin quivered and the vast spread of tail began to flex. The basking-shark had at last sensed their presence, was reacting with the beginnings of a swift, undulating movement.

Yogi Dunlop waited a fraction of a second longer, timing an approaching wave. It met the boat, sent it heaving, then he yanked the firing cord at the exact moment of the barrel's maximum depression.

Several things happened simultaneously. The gun's flat bang, the slamming underwater impact of the harpoon as it stabbed deep into the shark just ahead of that dorsal-sail, the initial whip of the harpoon line . . . and then the sea seemed to explode.

Surging out of the waves, almost twice a man's height in its size, a great tail lashed in a blind frenzy. The *Seapearl*'s hull gave an enormous shudder as it took a first then a second slamming blow just for'ard of the wheelhouse, blows which would have demolished many a lighter craft.

Thrown violently, Carrick grabbed for support as Dave Rother toppled against him and a solid wall of water hit the wheelhouse glass. The boat was still pitching and twisting like a creature gone mad, line snapping out from her bow, a great boiling patch of sea marking where the basking-shark had dived. From the stern came a tortured, erratic whine as their propeller blades briefly hit empty air.

'We're in him. Fair and sure. Got him and . . .' Dave Rother's shout of triumph died as he watched the line still vanishing overboard at express speed while the shark continued its plunge into the depths. The spliced-on marker barrel tore free of its lashings and disappeared in the same way an instant later.

'Where the hell's he planning to stop!' Rother scrambled to reach the helm again, suddenly tight-lipped. But as he got there the remaining line gave a convulsive wriggle, stopped running, and the marker barrel shot out of the water some thirty feet ahead, splashed down again, then bobbed idly.

Swearing, Rother slammed the heavy gear lever to full astern and ignored the protesting machinery noises coming from below. Spinning the wheel, he almost broadsided the boat to avoid running over the slack line, then, as they lost way, rolling wildly, he shook his head disconsolately.

'Gone, damn the thing. The biggest I've had the chance at, bar none.'

At the bow, Yogi Dunlop and Clapper Bell leaned sadly on the harpoon gun. A couple of deckhands were already hauling in the useless line.

The harpoon was still on its end. The steel barbs and half the head had snapped off clean, the rest was coated in black, evil-smelling slime.

'The bastard,' said Rother softly. 'He's down there laughing at us.' He glanced at Carrick and grimaced. 'Not my day, is it?'

Carrick shook his head with an answering grin then thumbed towards the compass.

'He might surface again,' said Rother hopefully; 'Maybe if we hung around for a spell . . .'

'Maybe, but we're not,' said Carrick positively. 'Portcoig, Dave. You had your chance.'

He almost added that the great fish down below had earned a chance too. But he doubted if anyone else aboard *Seapearl* would have seen it that way.

By mid-afternoon, when they passed Moorach Island to starboard, the sea was still running high and, despite a brilliant blue sky, a strong wind continued to whip at the rigging. Bringing the shark-boat in close, Carrick saw that salvage work on the wrecked *Harvest Lass* was already under way. She was beached on the ridge of rock as before but figures were moving on her deck and the seine-netter *Heather Bee*, which was lying at anchor a hundred yards or so out.

The sight jogged Carrick's memory. Turning over the helm to Logan, he went along to Dave Rother, who was lounging on deck near the stern.

'Dave, I was to give you a message from Sergeant Fraser. He'd feel happier if you weren't around Portcoig tomorrow afternoon. Not while John MacBean's funeral is taking place.'

'I don't go looking for trouble,' grunted Rother. 'You can tell him I'll keep my crews on Camsha. Or at sea.'

'Fine – as long as you mean your other boats,' warned Carrick. 'This one doesn't sail till Shannon lifts the arrest.'

Rother gave a cynical shrug and looked out towards the island. 'Shannon doesn't worry me. I'm a damned sight more concerned about Peter Benson. Maybe I can get an answer this time – do you think he killed your engine-room man?'

'Let's say it looks that way. I'd rather wait till we find him.' Carrick rested his hands on the shark-catcher's low rail and considered her skipper's thin, scowling face. 'Some people might say that if Benson didn't then you could be a candidate.'

'They might.' Rother took the reminder without concern then stuck a cigarette in his mouth and left it unlit. 'But they shouldn't say it too often – I've a high sensitivity threshold about some things.' He switched abruptly. 'Still seeing Sheila Francis tonight?'

'Yes.' Carrick raised an eyebrow. 'Why?'

'Old-fashioned curiosity.' Rother tongued the cigarette to the far corner of his mouth, adding cryptically, 'Have fun, laddie. Always have it while you can. Hell knows what's round the next corner.'

Marlin's grey hull was already alongside Portcoig pier when the shark-catcher finally plugged into Camsha Bay. It was close on 4 p.m. and another recent arrival was tied up near the Fishery cruiser's stern, a small-sized coaster with a green hull, white super-structure and a small black stub of a funnel aft. The Broomfire Distillery boat appeared to have kept to schedule.

Easing in towards the pier's T-end, Rother let his fenders nudge the thick wooden piles just long enough for the Fishery cruiser's trio to scramble over. Then the *Seapearl*'s engine rumbled, she spat exhaust, and her battered hull swung away, heading across for the island.

'Not a bad character to know, that Yogi,' mused Clapper Bell, scratching his stomach with one hand.

'Funny thing he was tellin' me, though. Just about every man Rother's got is some kind o' ex-navy – though a few o' them finished their time in detention barracks.'

Beside him, the leading hand grinned. 'Maybe he hand-picked them, sir.'

'Maybe,' said Carrick dryly. 'Well, check back aboard – both of you. Tell the Old Man I'll be along in a minute if he asks.'

He let them go ahead, then followed slowly, interested in the coaster. The *Lady Jane*, registered at Glasgow, lay with her hatches open and a radar scanner turning idly above the compact island bridge.

Loading was already under way. Her twin cargo derricks were manoeuvring a large stainless-steel tank aboard from a heavy truck waiting on the pier beside her. The yawning midships hold space gave a glimpse of stacked whisky casks below.

'No samples available, Chief Officer,' commented a dry voice above the clatter of the winches. Harry Graham's tall figure stalked out from the side of the truck and came towards him. 'If there were, you'd be in a long, long queue.'

Carrick grinned at the grey-haired distillery manager. 'Let's say I live in hope.'

Graham grunted, keeping an eye on the bulk tank as it lifted again. The winches stopped, the heavy tank swung gently for a moment, then the winch engines renewed their clatter and it began a slow downward progress towards the for'ard hold.

'You came in on the *Seapearl*.' It sounded close to an accusation.

'That's right.'

'The whole village knows why, of course,' said Graham, frowning a little. 'What happens to Rother now?'

100

'Captain Shannon's decision,' shrugged Carrick, then switched away from the subject. 'We passed Moorach Island on the way in. Your salvage team looked busy.'

Graham nodded. 'I had a radio talk with the skipper. They're fairly hopeful about patching up the *Harvest Lass* but the rest is like you thought. They're not so happy about refloating her.' He shrugged. 'I should go out myself – but I'm too busy here.'

'You're not wasting time,' mused Carrick. The bulk container had reached the coaster's hold and another truck was already bouncing its way along the pier. 'Why all the rush?'

'Tomorrow's funeral.' Graham watched the new arrival pull up. It was loaded with whisky cases and the man in the driving cab was Alec MacBean. 'I've rearranged the whole loading schedule to have the job finished by midday tomorrow. They'd stop for John MacBean's funeral anyway and afterwards,' – he gave a faint grimace – 'well, if mourning follows island tradition there won't be much work done. Most of them will find it hard enough to stand upright.'

Climbing out of the driving cab, Alec MacBean scowled around then headed towards them, a cigarette cupped in one hand. He gave a curt nod in Carrick's direction, then ignored him.

'We're runnin' behind schedule, Mr Graham,' he complained.

Graham pursed his lips apologetically. 'Back to work, Chief Officer, I'll see you again.'

'Try and catch the murdering devil Benson first,' suggested MacBean sourly. His mouth twisted. 'Not that anybody did anything when my brother got killed. But then he didn't rate – he wasn't Fishery Protection.'

101

'And he died in an accident,' said Carrick wearily. 'This is something separate. Anyway, finding Benson is a police job – and even then they'll need proof. Too many people are forgetting that.'

Both men looked at him sharply.

'You think there's any doubt?' queried Graham.

'Let's say I don't like the old approach of "Hang him now, we'll give him a fair trial tomorrow",' retorted Carrick with a degree of irritation. 'They'll find Benson. But I want to know more about several things going on here before I start shaping any opinion.'

Graham shrugged in silence. MacBean looked away, muttering under his breath.

'You don't have to agree,' Carrick told them curtly. 'Just remember I said it.'

He left them and went on down the pier.

Marooned aboard *Marlin* as officer of the watch, Jumbo Wills greeted his return gloomily while making a vain attempt to hide a magnificent black eye.

'The Old Man's gone ashore, Webb,' he reported. 'He left word he probably won't be back much before midnight.'

'We'll survive.' Carrick considered him with a twinkle. 'But what the devil happened to you? Don't tell me he hit you on the way!'

Wills glared at him balefully through the undamaged eye. 'It happened while you and Pettigrew were still out playing at captains,' he said bitterly. 'There was a wholesale brawl on the pier just after we got back – a bunch of locals and a couple of Rother's people who'd come over from Camsha. The Old Man sent me with some hands to break it up.'

'And?' Carrick inspected the eye more closely. It was a magnificent bruising, going from black through purple to a yellowed brown at the edges.

'Well, the moment we tried to stop them everybody started knocking hell out of us.' Wills's young face screwed up in a painful perplexity. 'Webb, do you ever have the feeling you're having a bad week, the kind of week you could have done without?'

'Like this one right now,' agreed Carrick with a grin of sympathy. 'Duck quicker next time. But what about the Old Man? He said he'd be here.'

'He was, till a police car arrived with a note for him. Then he went off in it.' Wills fingered the swollen eye tenderly then itched the skin below. 'There's a CID conference being held at Portree about Gibby Halliday's murder and they need him. But you know how that'll shape. Our beloved captain will end up having an expense account dinner with the Chief Constable.'

'On the Chief Constable, you mean,' murmured Carrick. 'Where's Pettigrew?'

'Ashore too. He came in with the Mallaig boat half an hour ago, moaned about it, then took off for the village.' Wills looked puzzled. 'One of the hands saw him there, talking with Maggie MacKenzie.'

'Then heaven help Pettigrew,' said Carrick dryly. 'If Aunt Maggie gets him on the hook he won't find it easy to wriggle off again.'

The second mate considered the possibility with a hopeful malice then grinned.

'She'd fix him,' he declared hopefully. 'Poor old Pettigrew.'

Early evening crept on with the wind moderating and the sun still beating down on the bay. Along the pier, more truckloads of whisky arrived beside the coaster and were taken aboard amid a constant rumble of winch engines.

Most of the time Carrick stayed in his cabin. It was hot down there, but he stripped down to vest and undershorts, then lay on his bunk, smoking an occasional cigarette and trying to think. He had a growing, uneasy feeling that he now knew enough of what was happening to be able to put the pieces in some theoretical kind of order.

Peter Benson had vanished, leaving behind almost everything he owned. Then, while Dave Rother hinted at some mysterious deal just over the horizon, there was MacBean's well-stoked hatred of the sharkmen, Fergie Lucas' equal vendetta and the odd contrast of Graham's refusal to be labelled. And so far two men had died. One by accident, another because he'd been in the wrong place at the wrong time.

How much of it really went back to the dead girl, how much of it belonged somewhere else? Or maybe the whole feeling really came down to imagination and that thump on the head he'd taken.

At last, when the hands of his wristwatch were leaving six-thirty, he gave up and rose. Splashing water on his face from the cabin basin, he used a towel then glanced at the mirror. A tired-eyed face stared back at him, complete with a dark stubble of beard along the jaw-line. Grimacing, he reached for his razor.

Fifteen minutes later, feeling fresher and wearing an off-duty grey shirt and dark-brown slacks, Carrick went ashore. Things were quiet at the village end of the pier and he walked along a little, sniffing the peat-smoke in the air and watching the dozens of gulls parading endlessly along the rocks near the water.

An empty whisky truck clattered past on the road, heading in the direction of the distillery. Then, moments later, Sheila Francis's little Austin saloon purred into sight and drew up beside him.

'Been waiting long?' she asked with a smile as he climbed in.

'No, just arrived.' He gave her a long, admiring look once he'd closed the door and settled back. Her hair was caught back by a ribbon the way it had been the first time they'd met. She wore a short blue linen button-up shirt dress, sleeveless, the open neck giving a glimpse of the swimming top below, the last few buttons left casually undone and showing her long, sun-tanned legs to firm perfection. 'Where's this place you're taking me?'

'Not far, but not many people know about it. I wouldn't if Maggie MacKenzie hadn't told me.' She set the car moving and glanced at him oddly. 'I didn't expect you to turn up. With all that has been happening, I mean.'

'Asking if I'm playing truant?' He grinned at the thought, lit two cigarettes, and placed one between her lips. 'Not particularly. Things are quiet for a change and there was nobody around to stop me. Have you seen Aunt Maggie today?'

'This morning. She ferried me across the bay to one of the farms – I've an expectant mother over there.' The Austin had left the village and was gathering speed along the narrow, climbing road. She drove in silence for a moment, then added suddenly, 'I'd another patient when I got back to Portcoig, someone you know. It was Fergie Lucas.' Carrick showed his surprise. 'I thought he was out salvaging the *Harvest Lass*!'

'No.' Sheila shook her head. 'He said he was having the day off, and I don't blame him. He had a fairly nasty burn on his left arm from helping put out last night's fire. It needed cleaning and dressing.' Taking the car round a sharp right-hand bend, she frowned as she used the horn to scatter some newly clipped sheep wandering ahead. 'I wanted him to make an appointment to have the burn dressing changed at the end of the week. But – well, he said something that puzzled me. That he might not be around by then.'

'Meaning he'll be stuck out at Moorach. Salvaging the *Harvest Lass* isn't going to be easy.'

'I suppose so.' She shrugged wryly. 'It's just that – well, the moment he'd said it he looked as though he wished he hadn't.'

Around another bend in the road they passed the Broomfire Distillery, a tight collection of modern buildings nestling in a fold between two hills. It was surrounded by a high chain-link fence, but the main gate was open and a truck was loading casks at the main warehouse block. Harry Graham's staff were working overtime to meet his new schedule for the coaster.

Graham hadn't mentioned that Fergie Lucas was still ashore. Carrick sighed. There was no reason why the distillery manager should have told him, but it might mean trouble later.

His eyes strayed to Sheila Francis again, noting the way the sun slanting through the windscreen was picking new highlights in her copper-red hair. He smiled to himself and pushed the rest from his mind.

Five miles out of Portcoig they turned off the road and began travelling down a bumping track which seemed to wind endlessly through a mixture of rock and heather and tall yellow broom.

106

Here and there the track was almost overgrown. The only sign of life along it was a surprised rabbit which flicked its ears and disappeared into the heather. Lurching and bouncing, the car travelled on then suddenly they were stopping a short distance from the edge of a cliff with the sea an expanse of blue below. To the left, the derelict remains of an old crofting cottage explained the track's existence.

'We've arrived,' declared Sheila then laughed at his expression. 'There's a path leading down, idiot. Like to bring that basket from the back seat?'

He collected the basket and followed her out. They were some two hundred feet above the sea, but a narrow ledge of rock hidden by a tangle of bushes started them off on a scrambling route which led down to a tiny, sandy bay. When they reached it, the sand was warm and deep beneath their feet and quiet wavelets were rippling in only yards away.

'Will it do?' she asked, kicking off her shoes.

'Aunt Maggie did you a major favour. People spend a lifetime looking for a spot like this.' Setting down the basket near the foot of the cliff, Carrick stared up at the rocks above. Nothing stirred. They might have been alone in the world.

He turned. The pastel dress was lying on the sand near the water's edge and Sheila Francis had begun wading out. Her black two-piece swimsuit, minimal in coverage yet practical, moulded to the curves of her slim, bronzed body. Thigh deep in the rippling water, she looked back, laughed, then tightened the ribbon tying her hair before she took a few more steps out and launched into a lazy backstroke.

Carrick stripped down to his trunks and followed her into the cool, crystal-clear water. She circled slowly till he reached her, then pointed to a rock jutting from the sea about two hundred yards out from the bay.

'Let's go out there. Now . . .'

The backstroke's easy rhythm suddenly changed and the water frothed as she set off in a pulsing, powerful beat. Grinning, Carrick took the challenge and started in pursuit. But the girl was faster than he'd expected. Halfway out she was still leading and he found he was having to positively churn along in his crawl-stroke. When he finally drew level there was less than twenty yards to go to the rock.

'Truce,' he gasped hopefully. 'I give up.'

She nodded, eyes sparkling, and they finished the distance together then clambered on to the rock. It was long, smoothed by time and the sea, and they explored it like children, finding a hermit crab in the pool near its base and some tiny fish trapped in another awaiting the tide's release.

At last Sheila Francis sat down on a ledge and smiled contentedly as he joined her on the warm, grey rock.

'Like my private island?' she asked, droplets of water still clinging to her body. 'You're my first official visitor.'

'That makes it even better.' He flipped a pebble at the water below and watched it splash. 'Any special rules out here?'

She shook her head and seemed to shiver slightly as he put his arm around her. Then, slowly, her face turned and her lips shaped to meet his own.

The sun was edging down towards the horizon when they finally started for the shore. Swimming unhurriedly, occasionally diving down to chase some small fish through the fat, dark green wrackweed below, they at last waded back to the soft sand of the bay.

There were towels in the basket, covering a coffee flask and some sandwiches. They dried themselves down, dressed again saying little, then Sheila Francis spread one of the towels as a picnic cloth and began to pour the coffee into paper cups.

Patting his pockets, Carrick swore mildly.

'Cigarettes,' he explained. 'I left mine back at the car. Got any?'

She shook her head and he glanced ruefully at the climb up the cliff.

'I'll be right back,' he promised and set off.

The upward climb was steep and he was breathing heavily when he reached the top. The Austin was where they'd left it and he collected his cigarettes and lighter from the front parcel shelf. Turning to go back, he saw something glinting bright over at the ruined cottage, noted several large gulls pecking and scraping at the fallen stonework nearby, and strolled over with a mild curiosity.

The gulls took to the air as he approached and circled overhead, keening indignantly. But the smile forming on his lips faded as he spotted a chromed metal tube half-hidden by a slab of masonry. Stooping, Carrick dragged the slab aside, saw the finned shape of an exhaust, then, suddenly tight-lipped, threw more of the rubble clear.

Front wheel smashed and handlebars twisted, the old motor-cycle lay with fuel from its tank a dark stain on the ground beneath. Remembering the gulls, he left it and crossed to where they'd been pecking.

When one of the gable walls of the cottage had collapsed it had fallen in a jumbled heap, long since a home for tall weeds. But there were no weeds growing where the gulls had gathered.

Carefully, grimly, he removed the top layer of masonry, then stopped, staring down at the result.

Peter Benson hadn't got far when he'd left Camsha Island. There were cuts and scratches on his young, lifeless face, but they'd nothing to do with the way in which he'd died.

That came down to the shotgun blast which had torn away one side of his skull.

Feeling sick, Carrick glanced at the circling gulls and knew their purpose. He replaced the stones, took a deep breath, then headed back down the cliff to Sheila Francis.

Chapter Six

When they came back together from the beach Sheila Francis took one long, silent look at the ruined cottage, bit her lip slightly, then turned away.

'There's a farm with a telephone about two miles from here, near the road,' she said quietly. 'I know the people.'

Carrick nodded. Down on the beach, when he'd told her what he'd found, he'd seen the horror on her face. But only for a moment. Then her nursing background had swept into place like a protective professional shutter.

'I'll stay. Get hold of the police at Portree and try to raise Captain Shannon at the same time.' He saw a protest forming and thumbed towards the setting sun. 'At the earliest it's going to be near enough dark before they get here. I'll take a look around while there's still some kind of light.'

She didn't like it, but didn't argue. Taking a deep breath, she glanced at the cottage again, nodded gravely, and went over to the car.

Left alone, Carrick stood for a moment, then began a methodical search of the ground around the tumbledown cottage, gradually working back towards it. Within minutes the hovering gulls had lost their fear and were settling again, pecking at the rubble, and he threw some pebbles to chase them off.

111

After twenty minutes all he'd succeeded in finding was a faint trace of tyre tracks where a vehicle had backed up close to the cottage. He threw another stone at a big, black-headed gull bolder than the rest, then crossed to the motor-cycle. From the bright metal showing around most of the damage, it had crashed on its side along a road surface. Some fresh grass and earth were jammed in parts of the front-wheel spokes near the hub.

Added to that terrible shotgun wound in Benson's head, it was enough to paint a grim outline. Leaving the inevitable basics of where, why and when – where had Benson been killed, why had it happened, when had it happened?

He glanced thoughtfully towards the mound of masonry where the youngster lay buried. But that part was best left to the forensic men with their tweezers and their little plastic bags.

It had been a well-chosen hiding place. A long time might have passed before the body was discovered. A long, long time if he and Sheila hadn't come this evening, if he hadn't left his cigarettes behind . . .

Sitting on what had once been a windowsill, Carrick brought out the cigarettes, lit one, and ignored the squawking, hovering gulls.

Suppose Benson had been killed before that fire on the fishing boat. Then why had someone gone to so much trouble to frame the youngster, trouble which had escalated to include killing a harmless character like Gibby Halliday?

Someone? The same tendril of doubt he'd known earlier crept back as he remembered his own brief, hectic battle aboard the fishing boat. There might have been two men, a simple way of accounting for that otherwise uncanny blow which had struck him down.

Two men.

He found himself wondering if Dave Rother could kill in cold blood. Wondering and having a good idea of the answer.

Sheila had been gone almost an hour and, as he'd prophesied, it was grey dusk before headlamp beams lanced their way along the track towards him. Another minute and the little Austin braked to a halt near the cottage, two police cars pulling up behind it.

As men climbed out of the cars Sheila reached him first. 'They asked me to wait at the road end and guide them in,' she explained quickly. 'Captain Shannon's here too.'

Shannon was already coming over, side by side with a large, bald-headed man in a heavy tweed suit. The other policemen, mostly in uniform, were unloading equipment from the cars.

'You're sure it's Benson, mister?' asked Shannon as he reached them.

'I'm sure, sir.' Carrick gestured towards the rubble. 'He's over there.'

'That upsets a few elaborate theories,' said Shannon caustically. He glanced at the man beside him. 'Including yours, Inspector.'

The bald-headed man nodded wryly. 'Detective Inspector Rankin, from County Headquarters,' he introduced himself wearily. 'All right, Captain. Let's take a look.'

Rankin led the way, Shannon close behind. They vanished into the gloom of the ruin, a torch glinted, Carrick heard the sound of masonry being thrown aside, then after another minute the two men returned together.

'Anything else to tell us, Chief Officer?' asked Rankin bleakly.

113

'Some tyre tracks lead up to the cottage, but they're faint. That's about all.'

Rankin shrugged and glanced up at the sky. 'Like to bet it's going to rain?' he asked of no one in particular. 'That's my usual luck. Or if they're killed indoors we've a heatwave.' He sighed. 'I'll start my people working. Chief Officer, if you want to take Miss Francis back to Portcoig now that's fine by me. But I'll want you later.'

'He'll be aboard *Marlin*,' said Shannon heavily.

'Good.' Giving a nod, the detective strode off towards the waiting group by the cars.

Sticking his hands deep in his pockets, Shannon grunted into his beard. 'Well, you heard him, mister. I'll stay and keep an eye on things here.' He switched his attention to Sheila, frowning. 'Once you're home, young woman, stay there. And my advice is you keep anything you've seen or heard to yourself.'

Her mouth tightened.

'I don't gossip, Captain,' she advised coldly. 'And I don't need orders – I'm not one of your crew.'

'No, you're not.' Shannon considered her again and gave a fractional smile in the gloom. 'Maybe we should both be thankful for that.'

He went off after Rankin before she could reply.

'Damn him,' said Sheila at last, still indignant. 'That came down to "Get rid of her and make sure she keeps her mouth shut".'

'And that's what I'd better do,' admitted Carrick wryly.

They went back to the Austin and got aboard. Another police car was arriving as they drove away.

For most of the distance back to Portcoig the road was empty of traffic. They passed the Broomfire Distillery, closed and in darkness, then, as if in answer to Inspector Rankin's prophecy, a light drizzle of rain began to fall.

Still making indignant noises behind the wheel, Sheila Francis switched on the wipers. Carrick said little until the first lights of Portcoig appeared ahead. But there was one question on his mind and at last he asked it.

'How many people would know about that beach, Sheila?'

'Not many.' She shrugged. 'Most of them would be locals, I suppose.'

'What about Dave Rother?'

She kept her eyes on the road but her fingers tightened lightly on the wheel.

'Sheila?' Carrick waited.

'He knows,' she admitted reluctantly. 'I told him about it. But – well, that doesn't mean anything.'

'Not on its own.' Carrick tried to sound convincing. But there were times when the sharkman could be his own worst enemy and this was certainly shaping up to be one of them.

'There's Harry Graham,' declared Sheila suddenly. 'Or even Fergie Lucas . . . or it could be someone else, someone you don't even know exists.'

Carrick nodded, but didn't answer. She looked at him again, sighed, and concentrated on driving.

Located at the east end of Portcoig's main street, the district nursing post was a small, neat cottage which served as living quarters and a treatment centre. Carrick waited till Sheila was in the cottage and the door had closed then walked slowly through the village towards the pier. The wind was rising and dark clouds overhead threatened more rain on the way. By the time he reached *Marlin* he was glad of the oily warmth which was waiting aboard and the hot, steaming coffee one of the duty ratings brought from the galley.

He found Jumbo Wills on the bridge deck with Clapper Bell. When they saw him coming they both looked relieved.

'Webb, we've a small problem,' said Wills sceptically. 'Clapper thinks we've had a prowler aboard.'

'I'm certain o' it, sir.' The bo'sun glanced scathingly at the second mate. 'Though some people think it's just a case o' too much beer.'

'What happened?' asked Carrick with a sigh.

Bell shrugged. 'I came back early – some o' the lads were talking about having a poker game. But they weren't around so I came up on deck for a smoke. An' I'm damned sure I saw someone in the water, swimmin' away from us towards the shore. It was just for a couple o' seconds, but he was there.'

Wills shook his head. 'Nobody else saw anything. Maybe it was a seal, Clapper.'

'A seal?' The bo'sun gave him the kind of glare he usually reserved for unpolished brasswork.

'Checked, Jumbo?' asked Carrick quietly.

'All I can,' shrugged Wills.

'Then leave it for now. Benson's been found.' He gave them a quick outline then glanced around. 'Where's Pettigrew?'

'Still ashore.' Wills moistened his lips. 'Look, if Benson was murdered then – well, who killed Gibby Halliday?'

'First correct answer wins a prize,' grunted Clapper Bell bitterly. 'Any orders for us, sir?'

'Not yet. Maybe when the Old Man gets back. But you'd better make certain most of the crew stay on watch till we know.'

Wills nodded. Scratching his chest, Clapper Bell looked out at the night.

'Bloody seals,' he muttered indignantly then lumbered away.

Midnight came round, bringing the last of the Fishery cruiser's shore-leave men straggling back from the village. Pettigrew was with them and Carrick stopped him as he made a bee-line course towards his cabin.

'Not tonight,' said Carrick shortly. 'You can get your head down later.' He considered the junior second with interest. 'Where were you anyway?'

'Making a . . . a social call.' Pettigrew gave an embarrassed scowl. There was liquor on his breath and his usually grey face reddened. 'Mind your own damned business.'

'All right.' Suddenly understanding, Carrick found it hard not to grin. 'But be careful – Maggie MacKenzie could eat you for breakfast.'

Pettigrew spluttered indignantly, the red flush spreading. Then he took another look around, the fact gradually registering that there were more of the crew around than usual. A sound like a groan came from his lips.

'Are we going out?' he asked wearily.

'No, but I'd be on my feet when the Old Man arrives,' advised Carrick. He told him why and Pettigrew swallowed on a yawn.

'Oh God,' said the junior second sourly. 'That's all we needed.'

For once, Carrick had to agree with him.

Captain Shannon returned at 1 a.m., bringing Detective Inspector Rankin and a subdued-looking Sergeant

Fraser with him. Summoned to join them, Carrick found the three men standing in a grim-faced semi-circle in Shannon's cabin.

'Close the door,' said Shannon heavily. 'Rankin, you'd better bring him up to date.'

Bald head gleaming in the cabin lights, the detective nodded.

'There still isn't much more, Chief Officer,' he admitted with a grimace. 'Our police surgeon won't be pinned down on what really matters, time of death. His guess is within an hour or so of midnight last night, either way. But try to squeeze it tighter and he just throws his hands up.'

'Mind you, the man's trying,' murmured Sergeant Fraser from the background. 'There's always the same trouble wi' a body found in the open. The overnight temperatures make a mess o' their calculations.'

'I hadn't forgotten, Sergeant,' said Rankin sardonically. 'Mind if I go on?'

Fraser cleared his throat hastily and looked down at his feet.

'Right,' said Rankin heavily. 'So the situation is that Benson could have been alive – or dead – at any time that matters last night. Then, somewhere, someone blasts him off that motor-cycle with a load of buckshot at close range.' He saw Carrick's questioning expression and nodded. 'The spread of shot tells us that much. And it was effective enough – the medical reckoning is he'd be dead before he hit the ground.'

'After which someone picked him up, added the motor-cycle, and drove to the cottage,' grunted Shannon. 'What's your chances there?'

'Damned few.' Rankin shoved his hands deep in his pockets and scowled. 'The wheel-marks back there were too faint to do more than tell us they were made by a car or light truck – even on wheelbase calculations they won't take us much further. As for finding a shotgun around here, they're almost ten a penny. Right, Fraser?'

The sergeant nodded warily. 'Most folk have one, sir. For game shooting or vermin ... I've known weans practically cut their teeth on the things.'

'So there we are.' Rankin crossed over to the cabin porthole and looked out at the night. 'Captain, I'd appreciate some help. Can you give me a boat and some men to take me across to that sharking base?'

'Mister?' Shannon glanced questioningly at Carrick.

'We're on full standby, sir.' Carrick paused. 'If you want, I'll ...'

'Not you, Chief Officer,' said Rankin softly, turning from the porthole. 'I've too few men available to refuse offers. But you've a reputation of being friendly with Rother. I'd prefer you to do something else, if Captain Shannon is willing. I've other men going to talk to this character Fergie Lucas and I'm sending Sergeant Fraser to see this distillery manager, Graham. I'd like you to go with Fraser.' He glanced at Shannon. 'Agreed, Captain?'

Shannon nodded but seemed puzzled.

'This car business doesn't fit with Rother,' he declared reluctantly. 'Damn it, he came over from his base by boat last night and went back the same way. That's positive – we had to sneak him along the pier to the boat when he left.'

'When he left,' agreed Rankin, unimpressed. 'Tell them, Sergeant.'

'The man has an old Volvo station wagon, Captain,' explained Fraser cautiously. 'Sometimes he leaves it in the village, other times over across the bay, handy for the island. He – well, he was seen driving it last night.'

Shannon's bearded face clouded. 'When?'

'Almost an hour before that fishing boat was set on fire,' said Detective Inspector Rankin. He looked pointedly at Carrick. 'Sergeant Fraser's regular patrol car crew were here in case of trouble when the pubs closed. They were on their way back to base when they saw the Volvo pass . . . which didn't matter then. But it does now.'

Rankin left minutes later aboard the motor-whaler with Pettigrew, two constables and a dozen of *Marlin*'s crew as a substantial back-up force. As the boat thrust off into the night, pitching in the heavy swell and quickly vanishing into the darkness and drizzle, Sergeant Fraser glanced almost apologetically at Carrick.

'Our turn, Chief Officer,' he said with a touch of reluctance. 'Ready?'

Carrick did not answer for a moment, still looking out at the night, wondering what kind of reception the motor-whaler's party would find waiting on Camsha. But at the same time he felt almost glad he wasn't with them. With a murder charge waiting in the background the task of questioning Dave Rother was one best left to strangers.

'Ready?' asked Fraser again.

He nodded, wondering briefly how the sergeant felt about having to handle Graham, then followed the man down *Marlin*'s gangway to the waiting car.

Like most distillery managers, Harry Graham lived beside his all-important charge. The journey took about fifteen minutes, Fraser driving with a silent, gloomy air and a savage disregard for the brake-linings. But he slowed as their headlights glinted on the Broomfire perimeter fence, then, immediately beyond it, he turned the car down a narrow lane.

The lane led to a small two-storey house which had a light still burning in one of its downstairs windows. Graham's car lay outside and the policeman coasted to a halt beside it.

Switching off, he glanced at Carrick. 'Better let me do the most o' the talking. I won't say I know how to handle him but – well, he's more used to me.'

'He's your inquiry,' said Carrick dryly. 'I'll listen for a spell.'

They climbed out into the drizzle and started for the house. The path to the front door was through a small front garden carefully netted against rabbits. The porch had an old-fashioned brass door-pull and when Fraser yanked it a bell clanged somewhere inside. After a minute they heard footsteps, light showed round the door edges, then it opened and Harry Graham frowned out. The frown gave way to surprise as he saw his visitors.

'Something wrong, Sergeant?'

'Aye. Can we come in?' asked Fraser.

Graham nodded, beckoned them in, closed the door, and led the way to a small study. It had some old sailing-ship prints on one wall and a work-lamp was burning over the desk, which was scattered with papers.

'Sit down, both of you.' Graham saw them settled then took the chair at his desk and eased it round to face them. 'I was finishing off some forms for tomorrow's coaster shipment, otherwise you'd have had to get me out of bed. What's the trouble, Sergeant?'

'That lad Benson has been found.' Fraser carefully balanced his cap on one knee. 'He was dead – shot in the head.'

Graham's thin face twitched. 'Suicide?'

Silently, Fraser shook his head.

'So you came here.' The distillery manager took it calmly but his lips pursed for a moment. 'Why?'

'I was sent,' said Fraser woodenly. 'You're not the only one on the list.'

'But I'm on it.' Reaching along the desk, Graham opened a drawer and brought out a small, framed photograph. He handed it to Carrick. It was a studio portrait of a young, fair-haired girl. She'd been trying to appear serious but the mouth looked very close to laughter. 'You didn't know my niece, Carrick. That's a good likeness. You'd agree, Sergeant?'

Fraser nodded. Quietly, Carrick gave him back the photograph and it was returned to the drawer.

'I've never killed a man without reason,' said Graham suddenly. He considered Fraser with a strange crinkle of a smile. 'You know that, Sergeant.'

'I know it.' Fraser moistened his lips. 'Some people might think you had a reason – or had found one.'

'No.' Graham ran a hand over his short, grey hair and waited.

'Then there's no reason why you can't tell us where you were last night,' murmured Carrick.

'At the distillery, at Alec MacBean's house, then at the pier' – counting the places on his fingers Graham glanced up – 'where we talked, Chief Officer, remember?'

'And afterwards?' probed Carrick softly.

'Here on my own. I went early to bed.' Graham's voice took on an impatient edge. 'Anything else?'

Slowly, Fraser unbuttoned his tunic pocket and started to bring out his notebook. 'Some names and times . . .'

'I'm damned if I will,' snapped Graham. 'If you've time to waste, come back tomorrow. But it's late, I'm tired, and I've a full day's work ahead.'

He got to his feet. Sighing, Fraser quietly fastened his tunic pocket again and started to rise. But Carrick stayed seated, meeting the distillery manager's glare.

'Tell me one thing, Graham,' he said softly. 'What have you got that's going to tell you who made Helen go off that pier?'

Graham hesitated.

'It would do no harm, man,' said Fraser quietly.

Shrugging slightly, Graham turned back to his desk, opened the same drawer again, and took out an envelope.

'I've got this, Carrick. It may matter some day.' He shook the envelope and a slim loop of fine, braided cord slipped to the desk and lay under the work-lamp's beam. A man's gold signet ring was on one end. Seeing the question in Carrick's eyes, he nodded. 'They found it round her neck, afterwards.'

Lifting the necklet, Carrick fingered the flat braiding on the cord, saw it was a complex mixture of reeving bends and sennet knotting, then examined the ring more closely. The signet face was a grinning skull and there were no markings on the underside of the shank.

'Nothing that helps,' agreed Graham harshly. Taking the necklet, he pushed it back in the envelope. 'A jeweller told me a ring like that would be hand-made. I asked him to find out more – he couldn't.'

'But you think you can?'

'I've patience for most things,' retorted Graham. His lips tightened. 'But not for all. I've shown you what you wanted. So now will you leave?'

Nodding, Carrick rose and the man saw them out. As the house door slammed shut behind them, Fraser started to walk back to the car.

'Sergeant,' – Carrick put a hand on his arm – 'you and Graham seem to share a few secrets. Maybe a few too many. How long have you known him?'

The policeman hesitated, then rubbed the thin line of medal ribbons on his tunic. 'Since I got some of these.'

'In the army, like Maggie MacKenzie's husband?'

Fraser nodded and smiled slightly. 'Graham, MacKenzie and a few others. Our whole unit came from this part o' the world.'

'And you all still remember it,' mused Carrick. 'Does Inspector Rankin know?'

'No,' said Fraser shortly, and started off.

'So between us we've managed to achieve sweet damn all – less, if that's possible.' Detective Inspector Rankin, seated at *Marlin*'s wardroom table, delivered his verdict with a raw sarcasm which wasn't helped by the way he felt. The swell in the bay had become a broken pattern of lumping, angry waves, the weather was building up, and he still looked green after a plunging return crossing in the motor-whaler. He considered the plate of sandwiches in front of him with open nausea. 'Captain, does this damned boat have to roll so much?'

'My ship . . .' – Shannon lingered on the word with a touchy emphasis – 'my ship is tied up at a pier, well sheltered, and all we're getting wouldn't disturb a sleeping child.'

'Have it your way.' Rankin pushed the sandwiches away and closed his eyes for a moment.

It was 3 a.m. and the wardroom atmosphere was an equal mixture of weary defeat and tobacco smoke. Standing near the starboard plating, Carrick balanced as the Fishery cruiser heaved again, heard her fenders rub the pier in protest, and saw the detective wince.

They had other company in the wardroom. Pettigrew was munching his way through another pile of sandwiches with noisy relish, Sergeant Fraser sat wrapped in a gloomy silence and a detective sergeant who'd arrived aboard looked almost asleep.

'I take it Rother wasn't particularly helpful,' murmured Shannon with a touch of malice.

'He made plenty of noise about wanting to co-operate,' said Rankin savagely. 'And made a pretty good job of looking surprised. But the rest was a double act with that harpoon gunner of his. They admit they picked up the station wagon over here and drove around looking for Benson.'

'But didn't find a trace,' grunted Pettigrew through a mouthful of sandwich. 'It's pretty weak.'

'Not as weak as our situation,' rasped Rankin. 'Anyway, that station wagon is being turned over to the forensic boys.' He glanced at Fraser with a chill disgust. 'And the same goes for Graham's car, first thing in the morning. Nobody can carry a motor-cycle and a dead body around without some trace being left.'

'Graham's car doesn't look big enough to cope with that kind of load,' mused Carrick, fighting back a yawn and not quite succeeding. 'What about Fergie Lucas?'

'He's been seen – and MacBean for good measure,' answered Rankin with unconcealed irritation. He pointed to the detective sergeant. 'Tell them.'

The man grimaced wryly. 'They're another double act. They say they were at the pier most of the night and they give plenty of names to back it up.'

'Sometimes MacBean uses one o' the distillery vans,' mused Sergeant Fraser.

'Then we'll check it like the rest.' Rankin winced as *Marlin* gave another roll and crockery clattered in the steward's pantry. Then, pale-faced, he got quickly to his feet. 'Let's leave it there for tonight, Captain. I – well, I've things to do ashore.'

Shannon nodded. 'And in the morning?'

Already heading for the door, Rankin stopped reluctantly. 'I don't know yet. I've got a car laid on to take Rother to Broadford Hospital – someone has to make a formal identification of Benson's body, and he might as well do it. I'll wait for him there.'

He went out quickly, the detective sergeant and Fraser following with mumbled good-nights.

Rubbing a tired hand across his beard, Captain Shannon watched them go then nodded to Pettigrew.

'You're off watch, mister. Webb, stay a minute.'

Pettigrew needed no second invitation and headed for his cabin. Waiting, Carrick eyed *Marlin*'s commander cautiously. When Shannon used first names, which wasn't often, it could sometimes mean trouble.

Bringing out his cigarettes, Shannon passed one over, took another himself, then accepted a light.

'You know Clapper Bell thought he saw a prowler aboard?' he asked suddenly.

Carrick nodded.

'I got the report from young Wills.' Shannon took a long, thoughtful draw on his cigarette. 'Then I saw Bell and told him to make a quiet check around. So far, you're the only other person aboard who knows that part.'

'Sir?' Carrick waited.

'Bell knew no one particularly believed him, so he was thorough.' Shannon's voice took on a note of tightly suppressed fury. 'One of the main power cable boxes on the bridge had been sabotaged. Everything would have been fine till we'd tried to

126

leave this pier – then half the electrical circuits aboard would have blown and left us helpless.'

Carrick moistened his lips. 'You didn't tell Rankin.' He made it statement and question.

'No.' Shannon smiled grimly. 'Mister, someone out there doesn't like us. Or doesn't want us to be able to sail in a hurry. I'd rather wait, say nothing and find out why.' He glanced at his wrist-watch and his expression changed. 'Well, now you know why if you find Bell going around with a self-righteous air. Just one other thing – I'll be ashore with the chief engineer for a spell in the morning.'

'Gibby Halliday?' asked Carrick.

Shannon nodded. 'Too many people seem to have forgotten him. But his wife arrives tomorrow, to take the body back for a family funeral. We – well, somebody has to be there.'

He stubbed his cigarette with a slow, weary deliberation, rose, and shrugged.

'Get some sleep, mister. You're liable to need it.'

Chapter Seven

The coaster *Lady Jane* began loading whisky again at 8 a.m., the racket as her winches spluttered to life crashing through Carrick's sleep and forcing him cursing from his bunk. Dressed and shaved, he ate a solitary breakfast in the wardroom then went out on deck.

The bay was a grey, greasy swell and there were layers of matching heavy cloud overhead. Along the pier, the coaster's winches rumbled again and more casks swung from the truck beside her. Then, as the sound faded for a moment, he heard a chuckle and turned. Clapper Bell was grinning down at him from the searchlight platform.

'Come on up,' invited Bell, sheltering a cigarette from the wind in one cupped hand. 'There's not much to see, sir. But at least you look down on it.'

Gloomily, Carrick climbed the ladder and joined him on the platform. Beyond the coaster, both sides of the pier were filled with fishing boats of all types and sizes, boats which heaved fitfully as the waves slapped their hulls.

'Heard the weather forecast?' asked Bell cheerfully. 'The met. boys say the whole coast is in for a right belting.'

The tied-up fishing boats made it certain. Whether they judged by the twinge of some sensitive corn, by hunks of dried seaweed or by the sheer 'smell' of the water, most fishing skippers seemed to possess a weather sense which ran well ahead of barometers.

The bo'sun yawned. 'Not that it matters much to us,' he declared. 'Hell, we look like bein' stuck here till the backside rusts off the old girl.' Taking a draw on his cigarette, he finished casually, 'I saw the Old Man when he left this morning wi' Andy Shaw. He said he'd talked to you about – uh – that seal I saw.'

'The one that fixed our bridge electrics?' Carrick nodded wryly. 'Some seals are pretty clever that way.'

Bell grinned. 'This one used enough copper wire for a knittin' pattern.' The *Lady Jane*'s winches rasped again and he glanced along then smacked his lips. 'That's a lot o' good liquor they're loading.'

Carrick didn't answer. He was frowning at one of the boats moored further along. It was the *Heather Bee*, though her salvage anchorage off Moorach Island should have given ample shelter from most storms.

'Some o' them will be in for John MacBean's funeral,' said Clapper Bell as if reading his mind. 'Never known a fisherman miss a good funeral – they should be bringin' that whisky ashore, not shipping it out.'

Absently, Carrick nodded then reached for a length of light line tied to the platform rail. Freeing the line, he borrowed Bell's diving knife, chopped a length off, then worked on it with care for a couple of minutes.

'Ever seen anything like this before?' he asked, showing Bell the result. It was as near as he could get to the strange braiding on the necklet kept in Harry Graham's desk.

'Somewhere.' The bo'sun's rough-hewn face scowled in concentration. 'It's fancy – a kind o' sennet knotting. I've seen it before, but not on any ship.'

'Then where?'

'Sorry.' Bell shook his head. 'Does it matter?'

'It might.' Shrugging, Carrick put the braided line in his pocket and left.

Jumbo Wills and Pettigrew were in the chartroom looking bored. He told Wills to stay close to the radio room, set Pettigrew unwillingly to work on morning rounds, then went ashore with a personal sense of frustration. As Clapper Bell had said, *Marlin* was just sitting there. The police might be busy but Fishery Protection's role seemed to amount to waiting without really knowing why.

'Webb . . . Webb Carrick.' Maggie MacKenzie's voice suddenly hailed him as he neared the village end of the pier. The grey-haired ferrywoman abandoned her conversation with a couple of fishermen and came over. 'I was going to come looking for you.'

'Why?' he asked.

'The Benson lad – it's all over the village that he was found murdered.' She looked worried, her hands deep in the pockets of the anorak she wore over her usual sweater and slacks outfit. 'I wanted to say I did see him like I told you that night.'

'Nobody says different, Maggie,' Carrick assured her.

'But it maybe matters a lot more now.' She pursed her lips. 'Not that any of the folk here are likely to admit they were wrong about anything. They're saying Dave Rother must have killed him, to keep the lad's mouth shut about something.'

'What's your own idea, Maggie?' he asked quietly.

She shook her head. 'I've none. I only know that Sergeant Fraser is prowling around like a frustrated bull. But – well, there is something else. When you asked me the first time about Helen Grant I said Fergie Lucas had been away at sea . . .'

'Six months, on the Australia run.'

'That's what he told people.' She hesitated, the wind ruffling her grey hair. 'One of the Mallaig boats has an extra hand aboard, a Glasgow man. He doesn't know Fergie but he's sure he saw him in Glasgow a few months ago.'

'You mean when he should have been at sea?' asked Carrick sharply.

She nodded. 'He says there was a fight in a bar near the docks. Fergie and a big Dutchman – and that Fergie got out just ahead of the police.'

'When did you find out?'

'Five minutes ago.' She glanced back at the fishermen who were waiting. 'The man's over there. You can ask him yourself if you want.'

Carrick considered for a moment then shook his head. 'We can check if Lucas did ship out. But if he didn't, Graham's niece was at university in Glasgow . . .'

'That's what I was thinking.' She pursed her lips. 'But I'll stay quiet about it.'

'Do that, Maggie. Anything else?'

'No, that's all.' Relieved it was over, she glanced at her wrist-watch. 'I'd better go. I've a ferry run due.'

'All right.' He smiled at her. 'And thanks, Maggie. How did you make out with Pettigrew last night?'

'Him?' She brightened and sniffed derisively. 'The creature fell asleep in my best chair, damn him. The world's running short of real men – ones my age, at any rate.'

Leaving him, Maggie MacKenzie went back towards the fishermen. Carrick hesitated, thinking over what she'd said, then went on towards the village.

Portcoig certainly knew about Peter Benson. He could sense it in the way small knots of people talking outside the few shops broke off their conversation and carefully avoided looking at him as he passed. The heavy, storm-threatening clouds above only added to the air of tension.

The village was uncertain what might happen next. But it sensed more trouble was still to come.

When he reached the district nursing post Sergeant Fraser's car was parked outside, empty. The cottage door was lying half-open, he could hear Fraser's voice rumbling inside, and he went in.

He found them in the back room Sheila used as a dispensary. The policeman was hunched gloomily in a chair and Sheila was perched on the edge of a small desk opposite him. She was in uniform and looked angry.

'Do I go out and come back again?' asked Carrick mildly.

'No, I'm going,' declared Fraser, rising with a sigh. 'I was only trying to do my job.'

'Then try digging for muck somewhere else, Sergeant,' she told him curtly.

Flushing, Fraser started for the door. Carrick stopped him.

'Anything new so far?'

'Ask Inspector Rankin when he gets back,' suggested Fraser unhappily. 'I'm just doing his damned leg-work – I don't get told why.'

He went out. A moment later they heard his car start up and drive away.

'Exactly what was that all about?' asked Carrick, puzzled.

'Dave – that man Rother, as our sergeant calls him.' Sheila moved busily around the room, still angry, packing equipment into her nursing bag. 'I should be out on calls by now.'

'Slow down.' Amused, he caught her by the arm as she went past. 'What about Dave?'

'He wanted to know how I'd describe what he called our "relationship".'

Carrick chuckled. 'Was that all?'

'All?' The air almost crackled around her. 'You didn't hear the questions!'

'Forget it,' he said easily. 'Fraser looked ready to curl up and hide – he didn't like it either. Anyway, it's my turn now.'

'What does that mean?' Her eyes narrowed dangerously.

'Tell me where Fergie Lucas lives when he's ashore.'

'Why?'

'Maybe I want to send him a postcard,' he told her, then grinned. 'Cool down. I want to check out an idea, that's all.'

Sighing, she crossed to a filing cabinet, fingered through some folders, then looked up. 'Lucas, F., 6 Glenside – that's a row of old cottages off the bay road. They should have been pulled down years ago.'

'Thanks.' Going over, he kissed her lightly on the lips. 'One other thing . . .'

'Well?' Sheila said it with a resigned sigh.

'Exactly how would you describe our relationship, nurse?'

He got out quickly as a heavy, well-aimed book just missed his head.

He passed Alec MacBean on the way back to the pier. In a dark Sunday suit, white shirt and black tie, MacBean emerged from a shop doorway still pushing a pack of cigarettes into one pocket. Their eyes met, MacBean gave a stony-faced flicker of recognition, and then the man strode off in the opposite direction.

At the pier, the wind was gusting a fine damp spray across the wooden boards and an emptied whisky truck which drove away had its wipers going to clear the fine coating of salt from its windshield. Aboard *Marlin* he found a few ratings working unenthusiastically at cleaning ship and Clapper Bell passing the time by resplicing the end of a throwing line.

'The radio's quiet,' commented Jumbo Wills sadly. 'At least, we're being ignored. *Skua*'s chasing a French trawler off Stornaway and Department are trying to raise a boat to cope with some Irishmen near the Clyde. But nothing for us.'

Carrick shrugged and glanced over towards Camsha Island, where the three shark-boats were small shapes tied in line near the slipway.

'Any sign of Dave Rother?'

Wills nodded. 'He came over by launch just after you left. There was a police car waiting for him.' He glanced at his watch and grimaced. 'Maybe we'll hear something when the Old Man gets back.'

'Maybe,' said Carrick vaguely, thinking over his own plans.

Leaving Wills, he went, found Clapper Bell, and talked to him quietly for a few minutes. At first Bell grinned. Then he looked doubtful, rubbing a hairy paw along his chin. But at the finish the bo'sun grinned again and went off whistling towards his storeroom den aft knowing exactly what was wanted.

After that, it came down to waiting. The weather stayed grey and gusty with Maggie MacKenzie's little ferry launch almost the only boat moving, bobbing and tossing its way out and back across the bay on a variety of missions.

The noon weather forecast was coming in when Captain Shannon returned with Andy Shaw. They drove up in a grey Fisheries Department car, climbed out at the gangway, and the chief engineer came straight aboard then went below as it drove off.

134

Shannon walked along the pier instead. Several minutes passed before he came aboard, and he beckoned Carrick to follow him. They went to Shannon's day-cabin, where he went immediately to the corner locker, took out a bottle, and poured himself a stiff measure of whisky.

'Thank heaven that's over,' he said with a note of weary relief, taking a long gulp from the glass. 'Help yourself, mister.'

Carrick did, then asked, 'How was Gibby Halliday's wife?'

'Quiet, too quiet.' Shannon shook his head. 'She's just an ordinary little woman, nice, plain – probably still trying to get hold of the fact he's dead.' He took another swallow from his drink then settled heavily in a chair. 'Anything happened here?'

'Nothing, sir,' answered Carrick and hoped he sounded convincing. 'The noon forecast is in – there's a westerly gale building up. But things have been quiet. Did you see Inspector Rankin?'

Shannon grunted expressively. 'Briefly. He says inquiries are continuing, which means they're getting nowhere.' He finished the drink and considered the empty glass with a scowl. 'I met Harry Graham along the pier just now. At least he's looking happy. The *Lady Jane* has finished loading, on schedule.'

'Before MacBean's funeral,' mused Carrick. 'That's how he wanted it.'

'He told me.' Shannon gave a cynically amused sniff. 'Not that he's taking any chance of her crew getting involved in the tears and sympathy boozing afterwards. The *Lady Jane* will be moving out soon, then anchoring in the bay till she sails at midnight. They may have enough liquor aboard to fill a swimming pool, but if they want a drink they'll have to swim back for it.'

135

'He's a hard man,' grinned Carrick. 'But why keep her there till midnight? The forecast . . .'

'He's more concerned she catches the tide at her next call.' Shannon found a few drops in the bottom of his glass, and sent them after the rest. 'Graham's idea of bedside reading is probably his company balance sheet. He's trying much the same thing with that seine-netter he hired to salvage the *Harvest Lass*. As soon as John MacBean gets his earth shovelled on she's supposed to go back to work.'

'Will you go?' asked Carrick.

'No,' said Shannon bleakly. 'I've had enough for one day. You can, if you want.'

Carrick shook his head. It was the last thing he had in mind.

The *Lady Jane* eased away from her berth at 1.30 p.m. and dropped anchor about a quarter mile out in the bay, rolling sluggishly in the lumping swell. Minutes later, as if her departure had been a signal, little groups of fishermen, all soberly dressed and without a jersey or seaboot in sight, began moving along the pier from their boats towards the village where other figures were gathering.

It was sheer bad luck that the police car returning Dave Rother dropped him at the pier gates at almost the same time. He came grim-faced along the pier on his own, met curses from the first group he passed, then slowed as the next approached and he saw Fergie Lucas at its head.

Viewing it all from *Marlin*'s deck, guessing what was going to happen, Carrick quickly left the Fishery cruiser and went towards them with Clapper Bell at his heels. But by then Fergie Lucas was blocking Rother's path. Suddenly, two fishermen grabbed

Rother by the arms and Lucas slammed his right fist twice into Rother's stomach.

Lucas' fist was coming back for a third time when Carrick arrived. Knocking the man's arm aside, Carrick pistoned the flat of his left hand hard into that grinning face. Swearing, Lucas staggered back while the men still holding Rother hesitated.

'Shove off,' rasped Clapper Bell, towering over them. 'Move, you maggots.'

They let Rother go and edged away. Lucas stayed where he was, muttering under his breath, right hand straying under his jacket flap and fingering the hilt of the sheathed gutting knife at his hip.

'Don't be a damned fool,' said Carrick softly, poised ready. 'The odds are wrong.'

For a moment Lucas stayed as he was. Then, reluctantly, his hand left the blade.

'Another time,' he said curtly. Then he carefully checked the knot in his black tie and went off, followed by his friends.

'Damn them,' said Dave Rother painfully, still nursing his stomach. 'Thanks, Webb.'

Carrick shrugged. 'Forget it. We'll get you back to Camsha if you want.'

'No need.' Rother drew a deep, wincing breath and straightened a little. 'Maggie MacKenzie's boat is in. She'll take me.' He paused. 'I haven't seen you since you found Benson.'

'They gave me another job.' Carrick said it neutrally, then asked, 'How did things go this morning?'

'Rough.' Rother's eyes smouldered. 'The mortuary first – which was the home-made psychological bit. Then that character Rankin trying to play cat and mouse again.' He paused then asked point-blank, 'Do you think I killed Benson?'

'I haven't heard anyone prove it yet. So – no, right now I don't.'

'Can I quote you?' asked Rother caustically. He nursed his stomach again and grimaced. 'Thanks anyway. I'll get on my way.'

'Dave,' – stopping the sharkman, Carrick pulled the length of braided line from his pocket – 'ever seen anything like this before?'

'Up to my neck in trouble and I should play sailor knots?' Rother stared at him.

'It could matter.'

Rother sighed, examined the braiding, then shook his head. 'No. Do I ask why it matters?'

'Not right now.'

'Have fun then,' said Rother dryly.

He nodded to Clapper Bell and walked on down the pier. Two minutes later the little ferry launch growled out, heading for Camsha.

Death's final ceremonial retains an old-fashioned dignity in the Scottish West Coast islands, a dignity heightened by rigorously disciplined simplicity.

John MacBean's funeral procession came past the pier at Portcoig at 2 p.m., following a route from his cottage home to the village cemetery on a hillside about half a mile along the shore of the bay. The motor hearse which had brought his body from the hospital mortuary at Broadford had been dismissed at the cottage. The plain oak coffin, topped by a single wreath, was on a low, open carriage pulled by two horses in plain leather harness, their heads topped by black mourning plumes which were whipped by the wind.

The carriage at other times did duty as a peat cart. The horses, carefully groomed for the occasion, were giant Clydesdales more used to ploughing on a hill farm.

Behind them came the traditional walking mourners, led by the parish minister, with Alec MacBean a grim-faced figure by his side. Some two hundred men, crofters and fishermen, shepherds and shopkeepers, followed in a procession which was four deep and which kept instinctively to the same orderly pace. It was an all-male procession – again that was tradition. Women mourned at home, those who wanted to visit a graveside did so later, when a bare mound of earth would hide what had gone before.

Clapper Bell was standing at the pier gates. As the procession wended past, he took out a large, off-white handkerchief and carefully blew his nose. Leaving *Marlin*, Carrick reached him as the tail-end of the mourners began to vanish round a bend in the road.

'He's with them,' said Bell with a faint grin. 'Up front in the second row an' looking as innocent as they come. So he'll be busy for a spell.'

Carrick nodded. Fergie Lucas was going to be fully occupied for the next half-hour – or longer, depending on the minister's graveside tendencies. The same thing applied to most of the male population of Portcoig.

'Got your toolkit?' he asked quietly.

'Uh-huh.' Bell tapped his pocket.

They set off in the opposite direction to the funeral procession, walking along empty streets where every window blind was drawn. Even the dogs were indoors.

'I know one thing,' mused Bell, glancing around. 'You'd better have a good story ready if we're caught.'

'You didn't have to come,' reminded Carrick. The edge of a blind twitched on the other side of the street as someone behind it gave way to curiosity. 'All I needed was the toolkit.'

'Leave you on your own?' Bell grunted disparagingly. 'Then you really would get caught. I'm coming – though I wouldn't if I'd any sense.'

They walked through the village and deliberately passed the isolated row that was Glenside Cottages. Fergie Lucas', number six, was last in the dilapidated line, which helped. Further on, reaching open country, they left the road and doubled back through a maze of thick gorse and old drystone dykes. At last they were behind a final drystone wall, only yards from Lucas' back door.

'I'll take it from here,' murmured Carrick. 'Keep your eyes open. Whistle me out if you see trouble shaping.'

He took the little toolkit from Bell, clambered over the dyke, and crossed quickly to the cottage. Then Carrick waited a moment. The only sound was the wind whispering its way through the overgrown garden.

Relaxing a little, he looked around. The back door was locked but the grimy window just beside it was held by a single snib-bolt. A narrow wafer of toughened steel from the toolkit eased the snib back, the window went up with a disused squeak of protest, and Carrick climbed through.

He was in a shabby, stone-floored kitchen which smelled of bad drains and stale food and looked like it hadn't been cleaned in months. The only other room held a few sticks of furniture and an unmade bed with crumpled, grubby sheets. His feet met an empty beer can and sent it rolling across the threadbare carpet.

Grimacing, Carrick got to work. Starting with an old chest of drawers, he searched carefully, replacing

140

each article as he'd found it. In one drawer he found Lucas' Merchant Navy papers. The most recent of them was more than a year old.

He moved on, checked through a corner cupboard, and he was going to close the door again when he saw a battered shoebox. Lifting the lid, he looked inside then pursed his lips.

The box held a collection of discarded oddments, from a battered silver cigarette case to a pair of broken sunglasses. But Carrick brought out the one item which mattered, a lifeboat whistle on a cord lanyard ... a lanyard braided in the same odd way as the necklet which mattered so much to Harry Graham.

The lanyard in his pocket, any doubts gone, Carrick left the way he'd come. It took a few seconds and another of the little pieces of metal in the toolkit to re-snib the window from outside, then he made the short dash back to the drystone wall, clambered over, and dropped down again beside Clapper Bell.

'All quiet,' reported the bo'sun happily. 'Any luck in there?'

'Enough.' Carrick brought out the lanyard. 'That braiding more or less does it, Clapper. If Harry Graham saw this, heaven help Lucas.'

'If?' Bell's rugged face twisted in a puzzled frown. 'You mean we don't let on?'

'No – not to Graham.' Carrick paused. 'But I'll need to get Shannon's help on the next part.'

'Just like that?' Bell stared at him in near horror. 'Then start prayin' the Old Man is in a good mood. That way he'll maybe only want our guts for a flamin' necktie!'

Shaking his head in despair, still not certain what was going on, he followed Carrick back through the bushes towards the road.

* * *

Captain James Shannon was in anything but a suitable mood. It showed in such danger signals as the way his stumpy body quivered with outrage as he glared at Carrick across *Marlin*'s chartroom table.

'Do you know there's a charge called breaking and entering, mister?' he demanded hoarsely, his beard bristling. 'As for this,' – he flicked a contemptuous hand at the whistle and lanyard lying between them – 'even if you're right about what it means we're talking about murder, not morals.'

'But they could both be linked,' said Carrick stubbornly.

Shannon's nostrils flared. 'Explain, mister and better make it good.'

'Fergie Lucas has been fanning trouble for Rother ever since the Grant girl died.' Carrick paused. 'Maybe just to keep his own nose clean – maybe for other reasons.'

'Such as?' asked Shannon sarcastically.

Carrick shook his head. 'I don't know, sir. But – well, suppose young Benson saw someone prowling on Camsha that night. Benson was on his own over there, so maybe he fought shy of tackling him. But suppose Benson followed that same someone back across the sand to the shore road, saw him drive off, and went after him on his motor-cycle. If he was spotted . . .'

'If,' snapped Shannon. 'And if again – if by someone you mean Lucas don't damned well pussyfoot.'

'Lucas then,' agreed Carrick without giving way. 'Lucas and maybe others. My guess is that's what happened. They saw Benson following, waited, and shot him off that motor-cycle. Maybe that wasn't what they meant to do. But it happened and all the rest was rigged, to make us think Benson was still alive.'

'And Gibby Halliday's murder?'

'You said it yourself, sir. He was in the wrong place at the wrong time. He would have spoiled everything.'

'It's still weak, mister,' grunted Shannon, unconvinced. But he looked more thoughtful. 'What about the police statements? Lucas has witnesses to say he was at the pier most of the evening. Even if they're lying, you saw him yourself – and that was less than an hour after Rother's sharks started drifting. There wouldn't be time to take Benson's body out to that ruin and hide it.'

'Not then. But there would be later,' said Carrick quietly.

Shannon sighed. 'And transport?'

'Would depend on who was helping him.'

'All right, I've heard worse.' Partly convinced, Shannon rested his hands on the chart table. 'I'll talk to Inspector Rankin, see if he'll run a full background check on Lucas.'

'And Alec MacBean,' suggested Carrick.

'All right. But Rankin isn't going to like it.' Shannon sighed again and shoved the lanyard and whistle towards Carrick. 'Better keep this for now. And you'd better remember MacBean claims he was practically in Lucas' pocket all the time. For the rest, we'll need to take it slowly. Agreed?'

'Agreed, sir.' It was better than Carrick had hoped would happen.

'Then it's settled.' Shannon prowled across the chartroom and looked out of a window towards the village. 'They're starting to come back from the funeral now. I want a positive check that Lucas sails on the *Heather Bee* the way Graham suggested he would. And I hope he does, believe me.'

'Something separate. The police have picked up a story that a mob of these idiots may cross to Camsha tonight and try to burn out Rother's base. Maybe that's why we had our prowler last night, to make sure we couldn't interfere.' Shannon pursed his lips. 'Well, they'll find out different. I've agreed to prevent any attempt to cross by boat. The police will take care of the road approach.'

Going over, Carrick saw the thin trickle of black-clad figures coming along the shore road.

'When will they try it?'

'Not till late on, mister.' Shannon smiled without humour. 'They've some drinking to do first. Then they'll talk about it for a spell. The time to worry is when the talking stops and the bottles are empty.'

It came down to watching and waiting, which was always the worst part. The slow hours, knowing that an invisible fuse could be burning through the sullenly quiet village.

Mainly quiet, at any rate. An hour after the mourners returned, two of the Mallaig boats sailed out. Their skippers were stern-willed men who herded their crews aboard under a combination of lurid threats and the size of their fists. An hour later, the *Heather Bee* followed them out of the bay through a squall of rain.

Fergie Lucas was aboard. More of a surprise, so was Alec MacBean. The erstwhile principal mourner wore an old sweater and dungarees like the rest of the salvage crew and was in the wheelhouse as the seine-netter nosed out towards her salvage job.

In the village, the rest of the mourners were too occupied to miss either man. Bottles and hip flasks circulating while they waited on Portcoig's two bars opening, they gathered in cottage kitchens, sheltered in doorways from the rain or simply wandered around, oblivious to the downpour. Glasses clinked while John MacBean's memory was toasted and the Camsha sharkmen were cursed in equal measure.

As the rain eased off Inspector Rankin arrived by car. Once the detective was aboard, Shannon ushered him straight to the day-cabin and the two men talked alone for some time. Then Rankin left, sour-faced, contenting himself with a grunt and a nod as he passed Carrick near the gangway.

'He'll check Lucas again,' murmured Shannon, coming beside Carrick. 'But he's not happy about it.'

They watched the detective climb back into the police car. As it drew away a drunken fisherman came weaving down the pier. He stumbled, fell, got up again, then unexpectedly went staggering back the way he'd come.

'One less to worry about,' grunted Shannon. 'There'll be more.'

There were, as late afternoon became evening and the weather stayed a blustering, rain-laced grey. A few times Maggie MacKenzie's ferry launch broke the monotony of their vigil at the pier, tossing its way out across the bay with passengers aboard.

One trip was different from the rest. The launch bucked through the waves towards the *Lady Jane*, still lying anchored in the middle of the bay. Harry Graham was the sole passenger. He stayed on the whisky-laden coaster about ten minutes then the launch brought him back again, almost disappearing at times in the spray.

Dusk brought the first real hint of trouble. Sent ashore with a couple of ratings, Jumbo Wills came panting back with the news that a mob of fishermen were gathering outside the White Cockade bar, which had just closed its doors for the night.

'They're on their way here, sir,' he reported breathlessly. 'I got near enough to hear them – they're planning to raid Camsha.'

Unimpressed, Shannon grunted, 'Half the stupid devils would end up drowned if they tried it.' He turned to Carrick. 'All right, mister, you know what to do.'

Ten minutes later, when a shouting crowd some fifty strong finally arrived at the pier, *Marlin* had quit her berth and was patrolling slowly about five hundred yards out. As she completed another turn and came back her main twenty-one-inch searchlight came to life and lanced through the gloom, pinning the mob in its beam.

'Listen to me.' Shannon's voice bellowed metallically across the water as he used the bridge loud-hailer. 'I'll arrest any man who tries to take a boat out. Understood?'

Fists shook and there were shouts of rage. But the rain, the wind and the occasional drenching spray helped decide the matter for the men on the pier. Gradually, still arguing, they drifted away again.

Scowling but satisfied, Shannon kept *Marlin* on the same monotonous patrol for another half-hour while dusk gave way to night and the moon came up, shining fitfully through the heavy, steady-moving cloud. Every now and again the twenty-one-inch beam swept across to inspect the pier.

It stayed deserted. Any belief that the Fishery cruiser might be disabled had been firmly squashed. And a brief message from the radio room completed Shannon's feeling of victory. Inspector Rankin's police road block on the coastal road had turned back four car-loads of fishermen – detaining two of the original drivers after they failed breathalyzer tests.

At 11 p.m. he ordered *Marlin*'s return to the pier.

She came alongside quietly, tied up, then lay with her diesels purring and deck lights blazing. But not a man aboard felt she'd be needed again.

'Take over, Mister Carrick,' said Shannon cheerfully. 'Better keep a skeleton watch on duty but you can stand down the rest.'

Then, making a noise which almost sounded as if he was humming a tune, the bearded little figure disappeared in the direction of his cabin.

Pettigrew took over the watch at midnight, while a clatter and rumble from out in the bay marked the coaster *Lady Jane* bringing up her anchor. She gave a short, farewell blast on her siren then her masthead lights began heading out for the open sea. Watching them, Carrick thought of the buffeting she'd take out there and was glad he wasn't aboard.

He was turning to go below when Pettigrew suddenly nudged him and pointed. A police car was coming fast along the pier, bouncing over the boards, its headlamps blazing. The car braked to a halt opposite the gangway. Jumping out, Sergeant Fraser came hurrying aboard and arrived on the bridge seconds later.

'How soon can you sail, man?' he blurted without preliminaries.

'Any time.' Carrick glanced at Pettigrew and thumbed towards the bridge intercom. As Pettigrew buzzed Shannon's cabin he turned back to the policeman. 'What's happened?'

'Maggie MacKenzie's boat is overdue.' Fraser moistened his lips. 'An' I'd better tell you now, Chief Officer. She's got Nurse Francis with her – they went out this evening to an emergency call across the bay. That was hours ago an' there's been no word o' them since.'

Carrick stared at him, feeling his stomach gripped by a sudden, chill fear.

'Maybe they're still over there,' he suggested hopefully.

'Maggie's no fool,' grated Fraser. 'She'd have got word back to someone before now – they've been gone three hours, an' the last thing she told her neighbour was she'd be back in less than two.'

'Where were they going?'

Fraser shook his head helplessly. 'Man, since I found out I've tried every home wi' a telephone across there. None o' them called for the nurse, none o' them have seen anything o' Maggie's boat.'

The sudden blare of *Marlin*'s alarm klaxon swung them round. In his shirt-sleeves, tie hanging loose, Shannon was standing behind them. He kept his thumb on the klaxon button for a moment longer then let it die.

'I heard,' he said shortly. 'All right, Fraser. We'll start looking. Get back up to the village and drag out any men you can. Some on the fishing boats, the rest along the shore – you know the drill.'

Fraser nodded but hesitated. 'Suppose they've drifted outside the bay . . . ?'

'Then, if they're in that eggshell, God help them,' snarled Shannon. 'Move, man.'

Nodding, Fraser spun on his heel and hurried down the companionway ladder. As he crossed the gangway *Marlin*'s crew were already scrambling to their stations and her diesel exhaust had begun to quicken.

Searchlights blazing, searing white magnesium flares bursting high above her at regular intervals, the Fishery cruiser combed her way round the bay with every look-out available pitting his eyes against the blustering, spray-lashed night.

Behind her, smaller lights were soon bobbing and twinkling in the darkness as the first of the Portcoig boats joined in the hunt. Hunched in the command chair, one ear tuned to the growing chatter coming from the VHF receiver, Captain Shannon stayed impassive as he gave an occasional curt order. His task was to employ *Marlin*'s potential in the best possible way. The rest he left to the oilskin-clad men being drenched on the bridge wings.

But as time went on he spared a grimly understanding glance at the two scuba-suited figures waiting at his side. Carrick and Clapper Bell had line harnesses clipped ready round their waists. If and when there was a sighting their turn would come.

'The MacKenzie woman knows her business,' said Shannon gruffly. 'Whatever's happened, the odds are she'll be coping.'

Carrick nodded silently then grabbed the radar mounting for balance as *Marlin* heaved and pitched round on another leg of her search.

They were halfway towards their next turn when an excited voice crackled from the radio, cutting across the rest of the searchers' chatter.

'West o' you, *Marlin*. We've got something. But we'll need help. Over.'

'Acknowledge, mister,' snapped Shannon. 'Ask for a red flare. Then get aft with Bell and wait there.'

As the red flare curved skywards, astern and near the mouth of the bay, the Fishery cruiser corkscrewed round on full rudder with her deck mats vibrating. Minutes later she reached the spot, close to the barrier of shoal rocks flanking the entrance channel. A small line-boat was heaving in a fury of broken water, her

149

feeble spotlight trained on an upturned red and white hull which almost disappeared in each fresh sea.

Creeping in cautiously, *Marlin* brought her searchlights into play, stabbing the night around. Fragments of wreckage tossed here and there. But there was nothing more.

Waiting aft, Carrick grabbed the deck phone as it buzzed.

'I'll leave it to you, mister,' said Shannon's voice in his ear. 'It looks bad. But there's always just the chance . . .'

'We'll check,' said Carrick greyly.

'On your own timing, then.' Shannon sounded tired.

Reclipping the handset, Carrick drew a deep breath. There might be an air space under that overturned hull. People had survived that way before. If there wasn't, then there might be a body.

Someone had to find out.

As *Marlin* edged in closer Carrick checked the safety line round his waist. Then, while Bell did the same, he made sure the deckhands beside them were ready. Nodding to them, he crossed to the rail, waited for the next wave to pass, then launched himself over the side feet first.

The cold sea met him like a numbing shock as he went under and he came up gasping, the line at his waist tugging slightly as it continued to be paid out from *Marlin*'s deck. He heard a curse and a splutter in the water beside him as Clapper Bell caught up. But the bo'sun signalled he was intact and they began swimming towards the wallowing hull.

Waves slammed Carrick's body and a fang of hidden rock grazed his side, tearing the suit. But he kept on, the safety line still trailing, and at last his hands grabbed the overturned launch and he clung

150

there, breathing hard. Another moment and Bell was there beside him while the launch heaved sluggishly in the white-foamed, spray-drenched night. Easing over, he tapped Bell on the shoulder, signalled he was going down, then let go and duck-dived beneath the hull, feeling blindly as he worked his way along its upside-down decking.

At last his lungs wouldn't take any more. Kicking down and out, Carrick surfaced among the waves close to the hull and it was Clapper Bell's turn. The Glasgow-Irishman's burly shape went under like a whale and stayed down for a long time. When he finally bobbed up and shook his head, Carrick knew they'd done enough. A double tug on the safety line gave the wash-out signal to *Marlin* and they began swimming back.

The search didn't give up. Another half-hour later *Marlin* had begun combing outside the bay, leaving the fishing boats to continue their attempts inside its shelter.

But one boat didn't seem content to leave it at that. She came plugging out into the heavier swell with a signal lamp blinking furiously from her wheelhouse.

'What the hell does that one want?' demanded Shannon impatiently, scowling at the lamp through the whirling clear-view screen.

'She's making "must come aboard", sir,' answered the duty petty officer beside the coxswain. He reached for their Aldis lamp. 'What reply, sir?'

'Damn whoever it is.' Shannon sucked his lips. 'All right, acknowledge. Tell her to come in on our lee. Mr Wills, reduce speed to slow ahead, keep steering way.'

As the Aldis lamp began clicking and the Fishery cruiser's engines slowed Shannon glanced at Carrick, who was standing near the after companionway with a blanket round his shoulders.

'Mr Carrick . . .'

Carrick didn't hear him. His mind was still back at the overturned launch, the rest a dull feeling of helplessness. For once, Shannon merely shrugged, then reached for the bridge intercom himself and ordered a deck detail to be ready.

The fishing boat came alongside with fenders out and her engine throttled back. Her skipper skilfully narrowed the gap between the two hulls, the fenders bumped hard and then, as the boat lifted on a wavecrest, two figures waiting on her deck jumped across and were grabbed by *Marlin*'s deck detail.

A minute later Sergeant Fraser and Harry Graham were brought up the companionway stairs to the bridge. Fraser, his uniform soaked with spray, was grim-faced. Barely recognizable in an oilskin coat and wool cap, Harry Graham stood beside him with his mouth in a tight-set line.

'Something wrong with your radio?' asked Shannon wearily.

'No.' Fraser glanced around. 'Where can we talk, Captain? It's important.'

'The chartroom. Take over, Mr Wills.' Frowning, Shannon slipped down from the command chair, signalled Carrick to come with him, and led the way.

Four men in the chartroom's cramped space was a crush, but once they were inside Shannon closed the door.

'Well?' he demanded.

Fraser moistened his lips. 'We couldn't use the radio, Captain – not for this. The *Lady Jane* is missing now.'

'The whisky coaster?' As far as Carrick was concerned it somehow seemed ridiculous. He stared at Fraser. 'Are you sure?'

'As sure as we can be.' Fraser fumbled for his cigarettes. The pack he brought from his pocket was sodden and he tossed it aside. 'Can I . . . ?'

'Here.' Shannon slid his own pack and matches across the table. He was puzzled and showed it. 'You say you couldn't radio. Why the devil not?'

'There's good reason, Captain,' said Fraser. He took a cigarette, lit it, and drew thankfully on the smoke. 'Very good reason, believe me.'

'Then spell it out,' said Shannon bleakly. 'The weather's bad, agreed . . . worse here than inside the bay. But anything the *Lady Jane*'s size is safe enough.'

'I didn't say weather, Captain.' Fraser exchanged a glance with Graham, as if seeking support. 'All I said was she was missing. That's – well, for want of a better word.'

Bewildered, Shannon stared at him. 'Then explain, damn it.'

'Aye.' Fraser drew on the cigarette again, as if for comfort. 'Captain, I sent men searching the shore like you asked. One o' them found a body newly washed up.' – he saw Carrick tense and shook his head – 'No, a man's body, Chief Officer. A man wi' his throat cut.'

'John Vasey,' said Graham in a low voice. 'He was the *Lady Jane*'s engineer. That leaves three men – the captain, the mate and a deckhand.'

'And that's why we didn't radio,' said Fraser grimly. 'That, and because it could explain what's happened to Maggie MacKenzie.'

Carrick grabbed him by the arm. 'What the hell are you trying to say?'

'I'll tell you,' said Graham wearily, pushing the wool cap back on his head. 'It looks like the *Lady Jane*

153

has been pirated. And if Maggie and the Francis girl are aboard you can blame me.'

'You'd better know something else straight off,' added Sergeant Fraser with a bitter edge to his voice. 'It could be your sharkman friend Rother we're after.'

Captain Shannon made a swallowing noise and Fraser almost managed to smile.

'Captain, you may have put his shark-boat under arrest, but she's not at Camsha Island. As far as we can make out Rother sailed that *Seapearl* out as soon as it was dark tonight, while you were still busy keeping the Portcoig men off his neck. What's more, he's got a crew aboard who might have been hand-picked from the worst o' that whole Camsha bunch . . . nine o' them.'

'I said spell it out,' rasped Shannon harshly.

Fraser nodded. 'First, I finally managed to find out that Maggie had taken the launch over to Malloch Head. The Francis girl had been called out to an old woman wi' some kind of heart trouble. The launch got there, the woman's family met them, and the Francis girl gave her some pills. They waited a bit, then left again for Portcoig before eleven o'clock.'

'But Maggie wouldn't come straight back,' interrupted Graham. He chewed his lip. 'She had a package with her, one I wanted taken out to the *Lady Jane*'s captain – some papers head office need. I took the package to her house just after Nurse Francis had phoned saying she'd need the boat.' He shrugged unhappily. 'So Maggie said she'd do the emergency run first then drop the package off on the way back.'

'Anything else?' asked Carrick quietly.

Fraser shook his head. 'Just that I contacted Harry once the engineer's body was found. Then suddenly everything seemed to fit.'

154

Nobody spoke for a moment while *Marlin*'s diesels grumbled underfoot and her hull pitched in steady rhythm with the lumping swell.

At last, Shannon made a noisy business of clearing his throat. 'You're saying that Rother – or someone – seized the coaster before she sailed. Then that Maggie MacKenzie arrived alongside to deliver that package . . .'

'And would know the crew,' muttered Graham.

'So they would have to hold her, and the Francis girl.' Shannon nodded agreement. 'If they sailed the *Lady Jane* on schedule and dumped Maggie's launch on the way out of the bay the rest fits all right.'

Carrick moistened his lips. 'How much is that load of whisky worth?'

'A lot, Chief Officer.' Harry Graham rubbed one thin hand against the other and hesitated, calculating. 'It's still at 105 degree proof. Broken down to bottling strength, the retail value should be around nine hundred thousand pounds – including tax. Stolen, looking for buyers, probably about half a million pounds. He wouldn't find it difficult to move, that's certain.'

Half a million pounds, maybe a million and a quarter dollars, hell alone knew how much in other currencies. Carrick's mind chilled at the prospect. It was a prize worth seizing, one the men concerned had already proved themselves ready to kill to achieve.

'If these women and the rest of the *Lady Jane* crew are still aboard . . .' began Shannon, then stopped.

The same thought was in all their minds. One body had been washed up, but others might still drift in. At the very least, five lives were in a danger increasing by the moment.

'Do your people know, Sergeant?' asked Shannon suddenly.

Fraser stubbed his cigarette and nodded. 'I called Inspector Rankin. He's organizing a general alert.'

'Right.' Shannon pulled open the chartroom door, a new snap in his voice. 'Mr Carrick, don't stand there like some kind of lost sheep. Get us out of this damned bay while I check some courses – I want emergency speed and full radar scan. Let's find this damned booze boat, wherever it is.'

Chapter Eight

Captain James Shannon liked to boast that *Marlin*'s radar was sensitive enough to spot a gull and tell what it had for breakfast. But for one small ship to find another by night in tumbling seas and among a scattered maze of islands was something very different.

So he gambled on what he would have done. Slamming her way through the blustering darkness, the Fishery cruiser carved a heaving course towards the south. Down there, beyond the 'cocktail-shake' islands of Rum and Eigg and Muck, lay a host of smaller, mainly uninhabited outcrops. They had high cliffs and deep inlets. A flotilla of coasters could have tucked away among them and been secure from the most thorough sea and air search.

The rest was luck, though the storm was gradually blowing itself out. Scowling in his corner of the crowded bridge, Pettigrew had been working the radar screen on its fifteen-mile scan. Suddenly, he muttered to himself, clicked over to the ten-mile scan, peered again, then beckoned Carrick over.

'This blip.' He pointed near the far edge of the screen. 'Anything we should know about out there?'

'No.' Carrick looked round at Shannon. 'Contact, sir.'

'Range and bearing?'

157

Pettigrew answered. 'Due west at eight miles. Bearing two-eight-zero.' He paused apologetically. 'A rain squall was blanketing that stretch, sir. It's just cleared.'

Keeping clear of the activity, Sergeant Fraser and Harry Graham glanced at each other. Graham moistened his lips but waited until *Marlin* was heeling round on the new course. 'If it's the *Lady Jane* . . .' he began.

Shannon cut him short. 'We'll find out first. You're forgetting that damned shark-boat should be with her.'

Checking again over Pettigrew's shoulder, Carrick shook his head. The screen showed only that single blip, one that seemed strangely stationary.

For twenty long minutes the Fishery cruiser shuddered and rolled through the lumping seas, closing the gap towards the radar contact which remained exactly where it had first been spotted. Then, at half-mile range, the twenty-one-inch searchlight's searing white beam lanced out and Shannon swore in surprise as it lit the scene ahead.

They'd found Dave Rother's *Seapearl*, the shark-catcher showed no sign of trying to escape. She lay bow-on to the waves, her decks almost hidden by the spray which broke from each creaming swell.

'What are they playin' at?' demanded Sergeant Fraser, puzzled. 'If Rother's tryin' some trick . . .'

'No.' Carrick had the bridge glasses trained ahead. He could see the taut hawser stretching from the boat's stern, ending in a makeshift half-submerged raft of canvas and timbers. 'They've a sea-anchor out. It could be engine trouble – and they've lost their radio aerial.'

That was only part of it. The *Seapearl* showed every sign of having taken a battering from the storm, and

158

the way sea and wind were continuing to moderate couldn't have come a minute too soon for her.

'Good.' Shannon considered coldly for a moment. 'Hold course but reduce to half-speed. Mr Carrick, signal them we're sending a boat. Then take a boarding-party over – and warn every man on it to be ready for trouble.'

Nodding, Carrick reached for the Aldis lamp.

The clacking signal shutter brought an answering flicker from the shark-catcher's wheelhouse. Still slowing, keeping the smaller craft trapped in the twenty-one-inch beam, *Marlin* came round in a gradual curve then stopped briefly while the rubber Z-boat was lowered and Carrick's party clambered down.

Engine snarling, the Z-boat pitched its way across while the Fishery cruiser began her circling course again. Blanketed by the spray, the boarding party had only an occasional glimpse of the *Seapearl* until they were almost beside the scarred hull. Another moment, another wave, and they were bumping against it and scrambling aboard.

'Hey there!' A massive, oilskin-clad figure lurched forward to help the last men up. Yogi Dunlop grinned uneasily at them. 'Good to see you. Good to see anyone . . .'

Shoving forward, Carrick grabbed him by the shoulder and had to shout above the noise of the waves.

'Where's Rother?'

'Aft – in the engine room. But . . .'

Carrick signalled *Marlin*'s party closer. 'You know what to do. If anyone gets awkward, sort him out.'

He left them to it and headed aft along the lurching, foam-creamed deck. The engine-room hatchway was ajar and he shoved it back then clambered down the iron ladder into the oily, dimly lit area below, an area still warm but with its machinery silent.

'Dave?' Grim-faced, he looked around.

'Over here.' Dave Rother wriggled into sight from a space under the engine block.

His hands and face were smeared with dirt and grease and he sat on the grating where he was, twisting a wry welcome. 'All right, you caught us. Just don't take the credit for it.'

'Where are they, Dave?' demanded Carrick sharply.

'Who?' Rother asked it tiredly.

'Maggie and Sheila.'

Rother rubbed a bewildered hand across his forehead, leaving a new black smear. 'Back in Portcoig, I'd say. What's the panic anyway? So I duck out of the bay when the boat's under technical arrest, but . . .'

'Dave, give me one straight answer.' Carrick moistened his salt-caked lips, already sensing Sergeant Fraser's careful theory had been wrong. 'What the hell were you doing out here?'

'Taking a gamble on the weather and chasing sharks – I lost on both.'

'Can you prove it?'

Rother eyed him cynically. 'Want me to turn out my pockets or something?' His expression changed. 'Anyway, why ask about Aunt Maggie and Sheila? What's happened?'

The boat took a sudden lurch as a wave larger than the rest pounded her hull. Loose tools clattered, they grabbed for support, and the lights flickered. As the shark-catcher settled again, Carrick came nearer.

'When did you lose your aerial, Dave?'

'Around midnight. The whole outfit nearly went under,' Rother answered impatiently. 'Now look . . .'

He stopped as the engine-room hatch slid open again. One of the boarding party looked down, saw

Carrick, and gave a slow, significant headshake. Then the hatch slid shut again.

'I said I want to know what's going on,' said Rother bleakly. 'And now, Webb.'

'You'd better,' agreed Carrick gloomily.

Deliberately, keeping to essentials, he told what he knew. Expression quickly changing as he listened, Rother swore pungently at the finish.

'So on that kind of evidence you came chasing me?' He gave a gesture of contempt. 'Well, it's my turn now – and you'd better listen. You know why we're stuck here? We lost the ruddy propeller. Clang – gone, like that, right in the middle of this damned storm. The poor old tub nearly upended before we got that sea-anchor out.'

'That's when you lost the aerial?'

'And a lot more.' Rother glared at him. 'We were helpless – and it was no accident. Somebody had it in for us. Fixed us so good it was almost permanent.'

Carrick balanced with another roll then frowned uncertainly. 'Dave, that prop-shaft was running rough before.'

'Rough, yes. But take a look – a good look.' Rother thumbed viciously at the underside of the engine block. 'There's my proof. And you're going to find it interesting.'

Working his way over, still frowning, Carrick squatted down while Rother shone a hand-lamp into the dark space beside them. A length of electrical cable ran from one of the engine's mounting brackets, vanishing beneath the block. But what made him peer closer, tensing, was the way the cable had been attached to the bracket. Someone had used a flat lashing of carefully hand-braided copper wire – the same braiding he'd seen twice before.

161

'You know where the other end of that damned cable goes?' demanded Rother. He didn't wait. 'Straight to the alternator control box. That means any time our engine was running the full output of the alternator was being pushed along the prop-shaft – pouring current like it was a battery terminal. Now do you understand?'

Silently, Carrick nodded.

The same thing had brought disaster to plenty of wooden-hulled craft. But usually by a combination of accident and neglect. The principle was simple enough – any electrical leakage aboard which found an outlet below the waterline could use salt water as if it was battery acid. The result turned any two pieces of dissimilar metal within reach into a miniature electroplating plant, stealing substance from one to the other.

Propeller glands, rudder pintles, even hull fastenings could disintegrate in the unseen, unsuspected process. Once-solid bolts could end up crumbling like so much grit. There were ways to hold back the process, but not against the kind of massive current which must have been attacking the shark-catcher.

'No sparks, no overheating?' he asked, squatting back on his heels.

'It didn't even change our ammeter readings,' said Rother bitterly. 'What about that lashing?'

'It's the same kind I asked you about.' Carrick pulled himself to his feet. 'Could your crew ride out the rest of this, Dave?'

Rother gauged the hull's pitch and roll for a moment then nodded. 'No problem in it now. As soon as the radio's fixed we'll jury-rig an aerial and get one of the other boats out from base to tow us home.'

'Could Yogi take over?'

'Easy enough.' Rother paused suspiciously. 'Why?'

'Because we're going over to *Marlin*.' Carrick stopped his protest. 'No arguments, Dave – not if you want to help find Sheila and Maggie.'

'Plus the character who fixed us?'

Carrick nodded. He hoped so, at any rate. But it might come down to whether they got there in time.

Back in the dry and warmth of *Marlin*'s chartroom they faced Captain Shannon with Fraser and Graham beside him like a pair of sceptical, sour-faced crows.

'I've listened, mister,' rasped Shannon, glancing briefly and icily in Rother's direction then returning to Carrick. 'You say Rother is in the clear, that we really want Fergie Lucas . . .'

'And that he'll be at Moorach Island,' agreed Carrick calmly.

'Where's your evidence?' grunted Fraser, unimpressed.

Carrick had kept that back deliberately till now. Reaching into his pocket, he brought out the whistle lanyard he'd found in Lucas' cottage and laid it quietly on the chartroom table.

Graham stiffened at the sight. Coming closer, he reached out and touched the cord. Then he looked up, his face suddenly ashen.

'Where did you get this, man?'

'In Lucas' cottage,' said Carrick, almost sympathetically. 'Graham, you were trying to trace a ring. I went after the rest of what you had, that necklet. Don't ask me where he learned it, but he uses that braiding like a trade-mark.'

'You said Lucas' cottage . . .' began Fraser suspiciously.

'To hell with how he got it.' The words came from Graham like a whisper while his fingers tightened round the lanyard till they formed a white-knuckled fist. 'Carrick, how long have you known?'

'Not long. Mainly since I heard he wasn't at sea when he left Portcoig. He was down in Glasgow – where Helen was.' Deliberately, Carrick switched back to Shannon who was waiting impatiently. 'Dave found the same braiding used to sabotage his prop-shaft.'

Shannon grunted. 'All right, mister. But don't try to tell me Lucas was thinking of tonight – nobody could calculate when that propeller was going to come loose.'

'He was just being bloody-minded,' muttered Rother, then rubbed his chin thoughtfully. 'Maybe that's what was really going on the night those sharks were cut loose – and why young Benson was shot.'

'When Lucas had Alec MacBean as his alibi,' murmured Carrick. He paused. 'Graham, whose idea was it to move the coaster out into the bay so early on – yours or Alec MacBean's?'

'MacBean's. It . . .' – Graham chewed his lip – 'it seemed sense at the time.'

'Like it seemed sense for him to go out on the *Heather Bee* the moment his brother's grave had been filled in?' asked Carrick remorselessly.

Graham didn't answer. No one spoke for a moment while *Marlin*'s diesels throbbed lazily underfoot and she rode with the swell. But the sound and motion, by their sheer lack of urgency, made each of them conscious that time was passing, time they could ill afford.

'So when do we do something?' demanded Rother acidly. 'Do we wait till someone sends us an invitation to visit Moorach Island?'

Shannon somehow swallowed the insult. 'There was only that salvage boat lying there when we passed – no other radar contact.'

A jeering noise came from Rother's lips. 'Hasn't anybody thought they've maybe sunk the coaster just off shore? They know things have gone wrong – but they don't know how wrong. That way, they've more chance – and they've a hope of getting at the liquor once things quieten.'

'No, they wouldn't – MacBean knows better,' protested Graham, still white-faced but following each word. 'Damn it, salt-water impregnation would ruin the whisky in those casks . . .'

'But not the bulk stuff in the tanks,' said Rother wearily. 'Would the tanks float on their own if they were set free?'

Graham grimaced and nodded. 'They're designed that way.'

'Then what the hell more do we want?' Rother scowled round, and then blinked.

The chartroom door was swinging open. Shannon had gone. A moment later they heard *Marlin*'s telegraph ringing and her diesels began to increase their pace.

'He makes up his own mind,' murmured Carrick, smiling slightly. 'We're on our way, Dave. Now suppose you stop howling and we try working out what happens when we get there?'

With little more than an hour remaining till dawn *Marlin*'s radar showed Moorach Island bulking in clear detail on the five-mile scan. The screen had the *Heather Bee* lying at her salvage anchorage and showed no other vessel afloat in the area. And the

165

storm had died, leaving the Fishery cruiser travelling through a sea which had settled to a moderate swell.

In the scuba storeroom aft Captain Shannon looked around him and appeared singularly doubtful at what he saw.

'Damn it, I need my head examined,' he finally exploded.

'Maybe, maybe not,' murmured Dave Rother. The sharkman wore a borrowed black rubber scuba suit and was buckling on the big twin-cylinder breathing tanks which went with it. 'But right now you can use me, Captain.'

'You think that helps?' asked Shannon bleakly.

'He'll behave,' promised Carrick grimly, buckling on his own equipment. It included an extra watertight pouch with a short-range radio. 'Just remember you're not freelancing on this one, Dave.'

Rother nodded, sobering.

Shannon sighed. With Carrick and Clapper Bell the only experienced frogmen aboard, Rother's offer to help – and naval training in scuba gear – had left him with little choice.

They went out on deck. Similarly clad, his air tanks slung over one shoulder, Clapper Bell was supervizing a group of ratings who were lowering a rubber raft over the side. Gripped by the Fishery cruiser's wash, it swung hard against the hull as it met the water and was held there by the lines securing it fore and aft.

'We'll go through it again, mister,' said Shannon heavily. 'I don't want any foul-ups – either way.'

Carrick spat on his face-mask glass, rubbed the saliva with a fingertip, then rinsed the result in a waiting bucket of water, the result was the best demisting process known.

'You drop us close to Moorach and keep going,' he recited. 'Then we've got till dawn. After that, unless you've heard otherwise, you're coming straight in.'

'Right.' Shannon pursed his lips. 'They'll have us on their radar now and they're going to see us sailing straight on past.' He paused. 'The next hour is yours, mister. For the rest of it, I'm banking on that boat being close enough inshore to have a radar blind spot to the north-east. I'll bring *Marlin* in again from there, but it will take fully that hour.'

'Anything else, sir?' asked Carrick quietly.

'Just remember they've killed more than once already. We're hoping Maggie and the Francis girl are alive – and maybe the rest of the coaster crew. But if they've got them they won't hesitate to use them.'

'Unless we get in first,' mused Dave Rother. 'Don't we get the "no unnecessary violence" bit, Captain?'

'I won't be there,' said Shannon. He turned on his heel and made for the bridge.

Normal lights burning, *Marlin* passed Moorach Island on her port side at less than half-mile range. To any observer she was coming back from some routine task, her radio was still silent.

But on the sheltered starboard deck aft the three scuba-suited figures dropped one by one down to the rubber raft alongside then rolled from there into the sea. They surfaced in line, came together while the stern wash of the rapidly disappearing Fishery cruiser clawed around them, then dived down and started swimming.

Leading the rough V-formation, demand valve clicking regularly while he settled his legs into a steady crawl beat, Carrick felt the first chill of the water pass as they travelled on. Now and again he checked his wrist-compass then glanced round to check the air-bubble plumes on either side.

They surfaced briefly after ten minutes, saw the *Heather Bee* now only a short distance ahead, then went down again. Occasional shadow-like forms flitted from their path in the dark water, fish giving surprised way to their passage. But Carrick's attention was on the wrist-compass, his mind locked on calculating their progress.

Suddenly Clapper Bell overtook him, nudged urgently, and pointed to their right. A darker patch of water showed above. Beckoning Rother to follow, they finned over, almost collided with the thin line of a mooring hawser, then surfaced quietly close under the seine-netter's bow.

Easing closer, hand-holding against the hull, they waited and heard voices. Another moment and a door banged open, the voices became louder, and a cigarette end curved its fiery tip into the sea. Footsteps sounded above, a man laughed, then a dinghy was dragged alongside by its painter line. A man clambered down into it, seemed to look straight in their direction, then calmly unshipped the oars.

Pushing off, he called a farewell.

'Just keep clear of the girl – she bites,' came the answer from above. It was Fergie Lucas' voice.

The men on deck laughed, then as the dinghy rowed away there were more footsteps and the door slammed shut again.

Edging beside Carrick, Rother let his breathing tube dangle and thumbed in the direction of the dinghy.

'Best bet?' he asked softly.

'Carrick nodded, signalled to Clapper Bell, and they began swimming again, heads just visible above the surface, making no attempt to overtake the oarsman.

Heading for the rocks where the wrecked *Harvest Lass* was a stark silhouette against the gradually lightening sky, the dinghy threaded past one jagged outcrop. Briefly lost from sight, there was a crunch as its bow grated against shingle, then a splash and more grating as the man aboard jumped ashore and dragged it higher out of the water.

Another moment and they saw him again as a match flared while he stopped to light a cigarette. Then he went on along the shore, heading in the opposite direction from the *Harvest Lass*.

Carrick waved his companions on. They waded ashore on the other side of the rock outcrop, quickly dumped their air tanks, then set off after their quarry – three wet, black-suited, almost invisible figures who moved in rubber-clad silence.

Three hundred yards along they reached another shoulder of rock, started round it, then drew back quickly. A glow of light was coming from a cleft just ahead and two figures stood at its edge. One, tall and thin, wore a grotesque home-made hood over his head. The man they'd followed was beside him, pulling on another.

'Jackpot time,' breathed Dave Rother. 'Let's take them.'

'Our way,' murmured Carrick. The tall, thin figure held a shotgun in the crook of his arm. 'Wait here, give Clapper and me ten minutes to work round, then draw them out.'

Rother sighed, but nodded. Touching Bell on the arm, Carrick took him back a few yards, then pointed upwards.

The climb was steep but the worn rock gave plenty of foothold. They reached a grassy slope, crawled along it, then found themselves looking directly down at the cave-mouth where the two men were still standing.

Clapper Bell grinned and they crawled on again. The way down, over another steep rock face, gave them one heart-stopping moment when a seabird exploded skywards almost under Carrick's feet. They froze where they were while the bird circled, screaming angrily. The voices at the cave stopped. Then, after a moment, one of the men laughed and the murmur of conversation picked up.

Carrick and Bell finished the descent to shore level, grinned at each other in sheer relief, then crept closer. When they stopped they were behind a great, broken slab of rock only yards from the hooded figures.

Carrick checked his watch. As the final seconds ticked past he nudged Bell and they tensed. Exactly on the ten-minute mark Dave Rother stepped out of hiding and began crunching his way openly over the shingle, whistling casually as he came.

Both guards swung round. Startled, momentarily undecided, they peered at him through the gloom. Then suddenly the man with the shotgun cursed and started to bring up the long-barrelled weapon.

Halfway there already, Carrick catapulted the rest of the distance and took him hard from the rear, one arm locking round the hooded throat. They went down heavily, the shotgun clattering on the shingle. Clapper Bell had the other guard down and Dave Rother was sprinting towards them.

But all Carrick's attention was focussed on his struggling opponent. Breaking free, cursing, the man kicked out wildly and a heavy seaboot smashed a numbing pain through Carrick's side. Before he could recover, the hooded figure rolled frantically over the shingle and reached the shotgun.

Scooped up, the shotgun's cannon-like muzzle came round towards Carrick – but at the same instant there was an odd, soft thud. The gun dropped again, the hooded man tried to claw at his throat, then gave a strange, gobbling moan which ended as he fell.

The hilt of Clapper Bell's diving knife protruded from the rough canvas of the hood. The blade had sliced through before sinking into his throat.

Skidding to a halt, Dave Rother stared down.

'My God,' he said softly.

Shakily, Carrick got up and looked around. The second man was sprawled face down, lying still. Sitting beside him, Clapper Bell gave an odd grin but didn't try to rise.

'Thanks,' said Carrick dry-lipped.

Stooping, he eased back a corner of the dead man's hood, saw a face he didn't know, then gradually realized that Bell still wasn't moving and that the bo'sun's right leg was twisted awkwardly.

'I've broken my flamin' leg,' said Bell with a touch of disbelief. He thumbed without rancour at the cause beside him. 'This stupid devil toppled us the wrong way.'

Going over, Carrick removed the second hood. This time the face revealed was one he'd seen around Portcoig. The man was still breathing.

'I only thumped his skull.' Bell shifted slightly and grimaced quickly. 'Hell – look, sir, toss me that shotgun. I'll just keep an eye on things from here.'

Dave Rother was heading into the cave. Carrick brought the gun over then followed the sharkman. For a few feet back the cave entrance was a narrow slit, then it widened abruptly and ended in a bowl-shaped area slightly higher than a man. A small kerosene lamp was burning on a ledge, its light shining on startled, almost unbelieving faces. He saw Sheila and Maggie, two men who were strangers in seagoing clothes, a third man lying still, then a babble of voices broke around him.

Grinning, Dave Rother had his knife out and was sawing at the ropes that tied Sheila hand and foot. Carrick did the same for Maggie, then the seamen. The third man, his head bandaged and his face ashen, barely managed to stir and move his lips in a feeble thanks.

When he turned, Sheila was sitting up and rubbing her wrists where the rope had left deep weals on her skin. She gazed at him thankfully, looking as if she wasn't sure whether to laugh or cry.

'How did you do it? How . . . ?'

'He's got a private crystal ball,' said Rother dryly.

'It should have worked sooner.' Putting an arm around her, Carrick helped her up. 'How about you, Maggie – all right?'

Maggie MacKenzie nodded, massaging her ankles. 'Just tell me where we are and who these devils were, that's all I ask,' she said angrily.

'You don't know?' Puzzled, Carrick glanced at the others.

'We don't know anything,' grated the older of the seamen. He turned to Sheila, gesturing towards the bandaged man. 'Miss, could you have another wee look at him - he's breathing worse.'

Nodding, Sheila crossed over.

'That's our skipper, mister,' said the second seaman, sandy-haired and with dried blood outlining a cut above one eye. 'When those yobs in hoods came swarmin' aboard us in the bay one o' them used an iron bar on him. Johnny Vasey, our engineer, tried to belt the louse wi' a shovel.' He stopped, moistening his lips hopefully. 'Did Johnny . . . ?'

'No.' Carrick shook his head. 'He didn't make it.'

'Webb,' – bent over the coaster skipper, Sheila beckoned him over – 'they're right. He's worse. How soon can you move him?'

'We can't – not yet.' He decided the others might as well know too. 'Listen, all of you. We only dealt with a couple of that gang. The rest are still near enough – and we're on our own till *Marlin* gets here.'

The relief on their faces faded.

'How long till she comes, mister?' asked the sandy-haired seaman.

'Under an hour. That's what we're hoping, anyway.' He waited as Sheila rose, then told her, 'Clapper's outside. He says his leg is broken. Dave . . .'

Rother nodded and went out with her.

'Now do you tell us where we are?' asked Maggie MacKenzie peevishly.

'Not far from home – we're on Moorach.' Carrick grinned at her surprise. 'Where did you think?'

'A lot further than that.' She shook her head, still openly confused.

'What happened to you anyway?' he asked. 'You took Graham's package out, right?'

She nodded wryly. 'And there was nobody on deck when we got to the *Lady Jane*. So like a damned old fool I climbed aboard and they just grabbed me. Then it was Sheila's turn.'

'We were all stuck into a cabin under guard,' grated the older seaman bitterly. 'Never saw as much as one o' them without those hoods – then, a spell after we'd left the bay, they blindfolded us, threw us on some fishing boat, and locked us in the fish-hold.' His fists clenched. 'I know what I wanted to do wi' them – but I don't argue against guns.'

They'd been blindfolded again before they'd been brought ashore. Maggie MacKenzie hadn't exaggerated. They had had no idea where they were or what had been happening.

'Who are they, Webb?' she demanded.

'Alec MacBean, Lucas and assorted friends,' he told her, thinking as he spoke, ignoring her snort of rage.

He had two injured men on his hands now, neither of them likely to be easy to move. The only sensible plan seemed to be to stay in the cave until *Marlin* arrived . . . and the sooner that happened the better. Mind made up, he opened the watertight pouch at his waist, brought out the little two-way radio then stopped and almost groaned.

The radio's casing was smashed, its transistorized interior was buckled. Grimly, he remembered the kick he'd taken on his side and tried the set's switches. Nothing happened, it was useless.

Swearing under his breath, Carrick threw the wrecked set aside then looked round as Sheila came back into the cave.

'I've seen Clapper – it's a clean break.' She looked pale in the kerosene lamp's light. 'Dave's looking for some driftwood to use as a splint. And I – I saw that man. The one who . . .'

'I should have warned you.' Carrick nodded his understanding. 'Anyway, we'll move Clapper in here now.'

'You mean we're not leaving?' asked the sandy-haired seaman apprehensively.

'Here's as good as anywhere,' answered Carrick bluntly.

There were no protests. Taking the two seamen, he went out to the beach. The second guard was making faint moaning noises and beginning to stir. Beside him, the shotgun muzzle resting inches from the man's nose, Clapper Bell relaxed a little.

'Shouldn't be long now, sir,' said the bo'sun cheerfully.

The sky to the east now had a positive edge of light. The hour Shannon had needed would soon be up. Nodding, Carrick hoped the rest of it would go smoothly.

The two coaster men willingly dragged the semi-conscious guard back into the cave, with orders to tie him. They'd hardly gone when pebbles crunched along the beach and Dave Rother hurried out of the grey gloom. He was carrying a few pieces of thin driftwood but he looked worried as he laid them down.

'We may have trouble coming,' he said bluntly.

Carrick tensed. 'Lucas?'

'Maybe.' Rother chewed his lip. 'I couldn't be sure in this light – and I didn't wait too long to find out. But I worked along to where we came ashore and there's something happening out on the *Heather Bee*.' Seeing the two coaster men returning, he lowered his voice. 'I'll go back and keep an eye on things.'

'We'll both go.' Carrick turned to the coaster men. 'Gently with this one – and when you've got him in keep that gun ready. We're taking a prowl around.'

'He's big, but we'll manage,' grinned one of the men. 'Ready, sailor?'

Bell grunted as they hoisted him up, then gritted his teeth against the pain as he was moved slowly towards the cave. Once he'd vanished, Carrick and Rother started off along the shore. They went carefully, conscious of the way every moment that passed was widening the band of light to the east and increasing the risk of their being spotted.

The tide was coming in too. At one point they had to wade almost knee-deep through a froth of gradually advancing water. Splashing out at the other side, Rother suddenly grinned to himself.

'Another week and I'll have quit all this,' he said unexpectedly. 'Makes you think.'

'Meaning that deal you won't talk about?' Carrick kept his attention ahead.

'Why worry now?' Rother almost slipped on a piece of damp seaweed, swore, then carried on. 'The crazy thing is, the credit belongs to Helen Grant. She was a geology student – you knew that, but it was also why we were together a lot. The first time she came over to Camsha she went wide-eyed then started chipping rocks. Then, after she'd checked with some of her university pals, I told her to keep quiet about what they said.'

'She'd struck gold,' suggested Carrick sardonically.

'No.' Rother chuckled. 'But almost the whole of Camsha Island is one big chunk of diatomite rock – fossilized, high-grade insect cake, the stuff the chemical boys use by the ton in everything from toothpaste to oil processing. I'm selling out to a London outfit.'

'Big money?'

'Enough to square what I owe. I'll see her family get a slice of it and . . .' Rother's voice died as Carrick suddenly pulled him hard down behind the nearest rock.

The reef where they'd dumped the air cylinders was just ahead and beyond it lay the little inlet where the dinghy had been pulled ashore. But the grey half-light showed two dinghies' and the air cylinders had gone.

While they still stared the unmistakable click of a rifle bolt reached them over the murmur of the sea. It came from somewhere near – and the shot which followed a second later smashed into the rock close to their heads, chipping fragments like miniature shrapnel before the bullet wailed off in a wild ricochet.

As scores of gulls began rising and screaming they heard a hoarse, dry laugh.

'Come out of there,' called Alec MacBean. 'Come out – and make it slowly.'

Grimacing, Carrick rose and Rother followed him. As they stepped out, four figures quickly closed in through the gloom.

Carrying the rifle, MacBean came forward with his thin face a narrow-eyed mask. A few paces to his left, equally watchful, Fergie Lucas held a sawn-off shotgun. Their two companions, dressed like fishermen, were armed with pistols and glanced round nervously as the slight wind rustled a clump of gorse further in among the rocks.

'Stay like that,' snapped MacBean. Crunching nearer over the shingle he stopped and swore softly. 'Rother . . . !'

'We all make mistakes,' agreed Dave Rother sadly. Next moment he grunted with pain and staggered back as the rifle barrel slashed him hard across the face.

'That's a start.' Wolfishly, MacBean savoured the long gash he'd opened down Rother's cheek.

'Leave it, Alec,' snapped Fergie Lucas impatiently. 'There were three sets o' those air tanks, remember?' He came up close to Carrick, whisky heavy on his breath. 'Where's your other pal?'

'At the cave – he likes the company there.' Carrick eyed him calmly. 'So much he'll shoot anyone who tries to interfere.'

Licking his lips, Lucas nodded and turned to the men in the background.

'You two stay near an' keep your eyes open.' As they eased away he stepped back a pace. 'That was a neat trick Shannon played, Carrick. But you're the one left holding the broken bits now.'

'What about the men we had on guard?' demanded MacBean, scowling.

'Forget them,' said Lucas with a casual disinterest. 'We've our own worries.' He considered Carrick again briefly. 'But they still did us a favour. We were expecting one o' them back, so when he didn't show up we came looking.'

'And found us.' Carrick shrugged wryly. 'You might as well know the rest, Fergie. *Marlin's* coming back.'

'Not for a spell. Our radar's clear – and when she does we'll be gone wi' you along for insurance,' said Lucas with a sneer. He shifted his stance. 'Rother . . .'

'Well?' Blood still oozing down his cheek, Dave Rother faced him with a weary expectancy.

'We don't need you. Do we, Alec?' Lucas nursed the shotgun, the breeze stirring his hair in the gathering light. 'And Alec has a little matter of his brother bein' dead to square.'

MacBean nodded, his eyes hard and bright.

'John was his usual, plastered as a newt,' mused Lucas. 'But a brother is a brother.' He took one hand from the shotgun and cuffed Rother hard across the undamaged cheek. 'I happen to hate your guts too, Rother. You've fouled things up for me – right through.'

Behind them, the two men in overalls were watching from the fringe of the rocks. One licked his lips, as if he knew what was going to happen and wanted it finished. Then Carrick suddenly had to fight to stay impassive. Something had moved a little way behind the man. It had been just a quiver among the gorse, but a quiver that was too isolated to be any waft of the breeze.

178

'So you're all set for another killing?' he asked, deliberately raising his voice a fraction. 'Benson, Gibby Halliday, the coaster engineer – all yours so far, aren't they, Fergie?'

'That's right.' Lucas twisted a bitter grin at MacBean's hasty mutter of warning. 'Hell, why worry now?'

'But MacBean set up the job.' The gorse had stopped quivering. Yet Carrick was certain he'd seen another flicker of movement, nearer this time, drawing close to the two pistol-carrying sentries. 'Well, who'd blame you for hoping it would be second time lucky?'

Lucas' mouth fell open and MacBean looked equally surprised. Even Dave Rother, nursing his bleeding face, stared at Carrick.

'Meaning what?' snarled Lucas.

Carrick shrugged. 'That Helen Grant was drowned just before the last bulk shipment of whisky was due to go out.' Carrick paused, knowing he had to goad the man to the limit. He was sure about the movements among the rocks now – and there was more than one man out there. 'You let something slip to Helen, didn't you? Enough to let her guess the rest?'

Breathing heavily, Lucas stayed silent but the answer was in his eyes and Carrick became certain about the rest.

'That's what you really meant about Dave fouling things up, isn't it?' He glanced sideways at Rother, who stood bemused. 'Helen wouldn't tell her uncle – not the way things were between you. But she warned you she'd tell Dave. And you couldn't risk what he might do.'

'Shut up,' hissed Lucas warningly. 'Shut up, damn you.'

But even Alec MacBean was listening as if hypnotized.

179

'Afterwards there was too much fuss going on,' said Carrick softly. 'So you had to cancel the first plan. But you were still lucky – her uncle and his ex-army pal were so busy trying to hush up a scandal that they covered up something worse.'

Suddenly and silently one of the men over at the rocks had disappeared. But his companion was too intent on what was happening to notice.

'Nobody knew, did they, Fergie?' Carrick felt his mouth drying but kept on. 'Not even MacBean, who thought he was running the show. But tell him now. What happened that night? Did she jump – or was she pushed?'

A strange, bubbling, animal-like noise came from Lucas' lips.

'Which was it?' taunted Carrick. 'You killed her, didn't you?'

'Yes, damn you.' Face contorted, Lucas swung the shotgun butt back like a club.

But there was a shout of fear from the rocks, a single shot as the second sentry went down, then, as MacBean cried a warning, figures were rushing forward.

Snarling, Lucas glanced back, then tried to bring the shotgun round again, his trigger knuckle tightening. Both barrels of the weapon blasted as Carrick sprang in and knocked his arm up. Dave Rother was wrestling on the pebbles with MacBean, the running figures were almost with them.

Using the shotgun butt, Lucas smashed Carrick back and turned to run. But after a few paces he stopped, staring wide-eyed at the tall, thin figure in that ridiculously over-sized oilskin coat who had appeared in front of him.

Harry Graham came forward with an impassive

face and his hands almost casually extended. And Lucas came to life again, reversing the empty shotgun, swinging it like a flail.

Except that Graham suddenly wasn't there. One swift, flickering sidestep took him clear. Then he gripped Lucas oddly by the neck and shoulder, spun him round, and brought a thin knee up at the same time.

There was a snap of bone and Fergie Lucas went limp, his head lolling. Silently, Graham let him go and he fell like an emptied sack.

For a long moment the distillery manager stayed where he was, looking down at the man he'd killed. Then he shrugged slightly and turned away.

MacBean was in handcuffs, the two others were being dragged over to join him, Dave Rother was grinning from ear to ear. Still dazed, Carrick realized Jumbo Wills was at his side and that apart from Sergeant Fraser, who was walking quietly towards Graham, all the men around were from *Marlin*.

'We hammered the guts out of those diesels,' declared Wills, still almost spluttering with excitement. 'Then the Old Man landed us on the other side of the island, because we didn't know what the hell had happened. And that character Graham – once he gets going he's the original invisible man.'

'I saw what happened.' Feeling as if a nightmare had ended, Carrick took the lighted cigarette someone handed him and drew on it thankfully. Then, after a minute, he saw Sergeant Fraser walking back alone, Graham was standing by himself, looking out at the sea.

'Sergeant,' – Carrick went wearily to meet Fraser – 'did he hear? About the girl, I mean?'

'Aye.' Fraser nodded slowly and glanced over towards his friend. 'I saw him kill two Japs like that

181

once. God, that's close on thirty years ago – but he hadn't forgotten.' He moistened his lips. 'I'd still like to call it self-defence.'

'You've a witness,' said Carrick.

Out at her anchorage the *Heather Bee* was trying to get under way, heading out. The sight didn't worry him. *Marlin* could take care of whatever men were left aboard.

He turned, beckoned to Jumbo Wills, and started off for the cave.

What Captain Shannon vaguely termed the 'tidying up' took the whole day long. And when they got back to Portcoig the real aftermath began . . . though somehow, in the middle of it all, Dave Rother succeeded in disappearing.

It was 3 a.m. before Carrick finally managed to get to his cabin and collapse in his bunk and close on noon before he woke with Shannon standing over him and shaking his shoulder.

'Had a good rest?' asked Shannon sardonically. 'Mister, I was beginning to think you'd maybe died under those blankets.'

Grinning, Carrick yawned and found his cigarettes. Then he realized the bearded, moon-faced figure now slumped in the armchair opposite was eyeing him strangely.

'Rother brought his scuba gear back this morning,' said Shannon suddenly. 'The air tanks were empty.'

'We'll get them recharged,' said Carrick. He got up, yawned again, and started dressing.

Shannon stayed where he was, lips pursed, oddly silent. Then, at last, he said grimly, 'The distillery people had a boat out at Moorach this morning, trying to locate where the coaster was sunk.'

'That should have been easy,' agreed Carrick.

They'd an exact position from Alec MacBean, corroborated by the rest of the hijack gang. The coaster had been scuttled in thirty fathoms of water less than half a mile off the island.

'It was.' Shannon chewed his beard. 'Mister, when they got there the whole damned sea was littered with floating whisky casks. Then they sent a diver down. He says he found the cargo hatches open, just open, mister. Not smashed, not damaged.'

Shirt half-buttoned, Carrick stopped and scrubbed his unshaven chin. 'But . . .'

'Exactly,' snarled Shannon. 'You explain it, mister. MacBean swears those hatches were closed when they scuttled the *Lady Jane*. And do you know how many of those bulk storage tanks they've found so far? Just two – both of them washed up on Moorach.'

Which left six missing – six times two thousand gallons of whisky, in steel tanks which would have floated as soon as they came loose.

Shannon rumbled into his beard for a moment then looked up. 'I'll tell you Rother's story of what he was doing last night. He said he used his other two boats to tow the *Seapearl* down to Mallaig for repair. He did – I've checked. But they took a hell of a long time getting there.'

'And the crews will back him up, I suppose?' mused Carrick.

'Every last blasted one of them – I'd bet this ship on it,' spat Shannon. 'We can't do a damned thing.'

Six times two thousand gallons, call it two hundred thousand pounds cash. And a scuba suit with empty air tanks. Carrick fought down a grin, wondering where Dave Rother had his bonus hidden.

'Mind if I go ashore, sir?' he asked mildly.

Hardly hearing, Shannon shook his head. 'Say hello to her for me,' he said wearily.

This time, Carrick grinned, Dave Rother might have the whisky.

But there was no sense in letting him get the rest.